Off Chance

felix chance volume three
j.e. pittman

For my Dad

Horseshoes and Headaches

IF YOU THINK I'VE got it all figured out: I don't. If anything, I've got more questions now than before.

And a headache.

The clock in my hands alive with infinite possibilities as it silently counts the unspent minutes, waiting for me to turn the key again — held now in the Magician's hand in lieu of the Fool I was.

Don't get me wrong. All of time at my fingertips... kinda nice. But it isn't going to bring my friend back.

The one I just met again for the first time, right before he died. Who was a stranger to me in this life, though he never treated me as such — hesitant though he was around me.

I mean, for good reason — I kinda punched him in the face the last time he saw me, I think it was the last — not sure, and only that 'cause I stopped short of murdering him where he stood.

Friendships are complicated like that sometimes — the good ones.

Two minutes to four. Had I used so little? I could just...

"No," I reprimanded myself aloud, putting the clock back on the shelf where it belonged. There were other ways.

"Yes," Molly playfully contradicted as she hopped up on my desk, folding one leg under the other. "What are we doing next?" Non-sequitur engaged. "Looking for a lost city? Tracking down treasures unimaginable? What?" Her chin rested on a propped fist, coming eye to eye with me — hers glistened like an addict. I sat quiet, considering — itching my nose.

"If it's unimaginable," I started, "how can you know what to look for?" Logic.

"*I* don't," she smiled, waves of newly-dark hair falling around her face. Heartbeat skipped. "That's where *you* come in."

I thought about it a second, but nah, too grandiose. I'd had my fill of so-called adventure for a few lifetimes. But that smile, so like hers...

"How about some lunch?" I offered instead, breaking eye contact I wasn't quite ready for.

"I guess." Molly popped off my desk. "Where to?"

"Left," I pointed right. Molly raised an eyebrow in question. "Opposite day, right?" I turned, walking backwards.

"Suuure," she slowly nodded once — humoring me. Spinning herself around, she joined in on my silly walk.

Immediately though, I fell flat on my ass — heel catching a loose board I'd not seen because I was indeed being silly — and Molly came tumbling after with an oof and a gyah and a variety of noises a few octaves higher.

Achoo.

I ignored it. Preferring to feel Molly's weight on my bones.

"Maybe we should just walk normal?" Molly humphed herself up, brushing off her rear.

"Fine, fine," I capitulated as I stood, making a show of walking the right way round. "If we must. After you," I swept a bow forward — keeping an ear out for more sneezes.

"Oh no, no," Molly mocked, "after you!" Her wicked smile lit in her eyes — mischief in the making.

Hop and a skip, and what do we do?

"Fine fine," I hooked my elbow. "Together then?"

Molly cocked her head back with a laugh and looped her arm through mine. The warmth of her beside me as we walked felt good. Felt... familiar.

"You still haven't said where we're going," she broke the comfortable silence.

"Oh, that's quite simple," I said. "Somewhere we don't have to make the food. Tastes much better that way." I nodded my best sagacious nod.

"So, no Mallorey's," Molly pined. "That was fun," she perked, remembering our first con.

"Well, being as it's several states away," I started, "and that, last I saw, it was being repossessed piecemeal..." I shrugged as I trailed off — recalling the knife flicked out to cut the caulk from the running kitchen sink in Mallorey's. I'd run, too.

Achoo!

Not now, I didn't say aloud. Outwardly ignoring the summons.

"Sure," she laughed, "but there's bound to be other Mallorey's out there just waiting for us!"

I highly doubted it, though kept that from my face, instead plastering on a look that was apparently enticing, because Molly pulled in tighter, pressing her hip against mine.

"Molls," I tried to rile her.

"Hmm," she didn't snap. No customary *don't call me that,* followed by a disgusted glare. Rather, she seemed content.

Confusion set in, but before my forebrain could react, my feet danced us away from the piano falling from the eighth-story window above us.

Ain't that a sight?

Ivories I'd once tickled flying haphazard as the steel strings snapped in crescendoed discordance. The black-finished boards — lacquer, I think — splintered, revealing naked shards of the wooden upright brought low by the forces of gravity as they sprayed across the pavement. The tip jar that had once gracefully accepted gratuities atop it rolled off into the street — miraculously unscathed.

"What the actual..." Molly stared at the shattered remains in shock for a moment, clinging close for balance, before turning to see from whence it came. That moment allowed the looming shadow to flee into the eighth-storied window and escape sight as she railed. "Careful, you feckless twats! We're walkin' here!"

But I'd seen.

Wish I hadn't.

I mean, really wish I hadn't seen the slender tail slip over the masonry sill of the window.

"Can you believe that?" Molly was staring at me expectantly — waiting for me to rise to her level of indignant rage at the near death experience. Meanwhile, I was dwelling on the shadowed wings I also wished I hadn't seen tuck from sight.

"I mean," I shrugged, pushing thoughts from my head, "you wanted adventure," I glibbed.

"*That* is not adventure," Molly jabbed a finger at the debris. "*That* is straight from a cartoon."

"And it never hurts them either," I winked, faking some swagger. "C'mon," I took her hand, "I'm hungry."

Not far off I found a suspiciously placed eatery exactly as I expected I would — a hop and a skip up Northland Street.

Well, *eatery* might not be the proper word for it. I considered alternatives as we stood outside *Oh! Mademoiselle,* staring up at the top-hat-clad hottie on the poster who wore nothing save for strategically placed gloved hands and some dangling earrings.

"Why'd you bring me to a strip club?" Molly eyed the poster with slight offense. Strange. Tits had never bothered her before. Maybe the building wasn't up to code?

"It's a cabaret," I defended. "And, see? They serve food," and maybe some answers, I didn't say as I directed her glare to the banner beside the poster, which read '$10 Lobster Dinner!' Very emphatic, the banner.

"I don't think that's *food,* exactly, Felix," she doubted. "More like salmonella in a shell with listeria sauce." Her face greened a bit at the thought, gagging slightly. I could almost feel the bile sympathetically rising in the back of my own throat. Yum.

I rapped on the door three times. "They probably have wings, too," I mused, turning my back to the door. My fist pounded once, down low — finishing the knock just as I'd been shown by the parroted man, once, long ago.

The door creaked, cracking open just enough for a single eyeball and half a nose to appear in shadow.

"Whayouwan??" The giant who answered ran the words together as if they couldn't all fit through his grit teeth at once.

"Nothing, thanks," Molly sweeted, batting eyelashes as she backed away defensively. "Let's go," she mouthed.

"Trust me," I uttered, holding her hand fast. "Is Sean around?" I put on my least offensive face for the bouncer. The one I used when I wanted to engender goodwill and convey that in no way, shape, or form was I utterly untrustworthy.

"Pretty round," the giant chuckled, swinging the door open just enough for us to slide in.

"Felix?" Molly hesitated before relenting with a sigh. I squeezed her hand reassuringly.

Inside, neither wing nor tit to be seen - contrary to Molly's misgivings. There weren't any diseases masquerading as shellfish, either.

"See?" I turned in time to see Molly work her mouth agape as she took in the red velvet surroundings.

Plush booths divided by rich curtains and black-lacquered screens worked in medieval motifs — here a dragon, gryphon on the next. Scenes straight from the marginalia — one featured a fully armored knight charging, of all things, a snail. Sometimes I think those monks were tripping on the moldy bread they ate, scribing away in the near-dark.

"Hi sweetie," a nice lady beamed from the back booth. At least, I think she was nice. Had that favorite aunty aura — the one who never had kids of her own but took in all the strays. She'd feed you more than you could possibly eat, send you home with two plates, and bend the world backward to help you. And if you unwisely crossed her, well, she'd bless your heart — with all the associated connotations and consequences therewith.

I knew who she was, but hadn't ever — to my spotty recollection — made her acquaintance, and already I felt like one of the family. Odd feeling, that.

"Goff," she addressed the giant lurking behind us, "be a doll? They look all skin and bones. Sit," she waved.

"Not the lobster," Molly interjected before remembering her manners, "please." She creaked awkwardly on the leather bench, obviously discomfited.

"What lobster, sweetie?" Our new favorite aunty befuddled before us, eyes widening to fill her round spectacles as our concerns gained her full attention.

"On the sign," Molly hooked a thumb over her shoulder the way we came, "flapping and snapping outside, offering ten-dollar lobster."

"Who on earth would pay *ten dollars* for a lobster?" She made a sour face. "Those critters aren't worth half-a-cent even as bait! Ten whole dollars…" she trailed.

"I know, right," Molly reflexively agreed before fully processing, "…wait what?"

"Who's flimflamming people with lobster?" She laughed. "Give us some of that graft, hey?" She looked up at Goff as he returned with plates of not-lobster while Molly sat sorting out the words she'd just heard.

"Yuck," or something like it slipped through cracking teeth of the giant dishing out the vittles.

I couldn't tell what it was, exactly — some sort of meat and veggies plate — but it looked good. And more importantly, someone else had made it for me. I don't recall ever being particularly picky or paying that much attention, really. So long as it didn't kill me.

"Felix!" an interruption called before I could even take a bite. "I'm so glad you're here!" Damnit. I squeezed my eyes shut as the tinkly voice grate up my spine.

I had a question to ask the books our host kept, and now I-refuse-to-call-her-Helena sauntered in to futz it all up. Bubbly and sweet, she swept past the giant Goff to join our little party. Some bouncer he was.

"Sorry," I grimaced, "wrong guy." Doing my best to ignore the intrusion, I began looking for an out. The kind-eyed woman across from me was absolutely no help as she sat there sipping her tea Kermit style. Gee, thanks aunty.

"And who are you?" Molly chimed brightly at the competing effervescence — anachronistic lobsters now forgotten. I got the image of raised hackles from both, belying the sparkles each routinely emanated.

"I'm Helena," not-calling-her-that stuck out a white-gloved hand.

"Not-Helena," I grumbled.

"Why you can never call me by my name..." She side-eyed as Molly took her hand for a shake.

"Another one of your strumpets, Felix?" Molly's eyebrow arched accusatorially.

"Never," I defended as not-Helena was like, "Ew, no!"

"Excuse me," I glared, "'*ew?*'" My eyebrow quirked. Bit of an overreact there.

"You're like my little brother," she gagged for effect. "But in a good way," she tried to turn it around with a fake big smile.

Uh-huh, my eyes said as my mouth asked, "Why are you here?"

"I need your help, come on," you-know-who tugged my sleeve as she bounced up. "We've got a tower to sell."

Well, it *was* a tower, alright, I pontificated as we stood beneath the one Gus built as tourists gaped and golluped at the dark iron structure decked in sparkling lights.

"You're selling the Eiffel Tower?" Molly with the obvious, seeming impressed with the audaciousness of my former teacher-slash-student — it was complicated.

"No," Helena-so-she-said scoffed, "too easy. Been done a dozen times a dozen ways." She waved off the tacky thought before it could stick — tarnishing her criminal brilliance. The Saffron School prides itself on originality when it comes to *big* cons. "Just the lights," she smiled as she set off for a hapless tourist wielding an overly large camera. "Monsieur? Excusez-moi monsieur…" she accosted him in perfect French.

I watched as she fluidly switched her mannerisms to that of a haughty French bureaucrat waving about papers that no doubt looked oh-so-official. Poor schmuck had no idea…

"What's she saying?" Molly, too, watched the con unfold as Helena-wasn't-her-name-o worked her mark.

"Lots of words," I smarmed. "Most sound French," completing my smartassery as the silver-haired artiste accepted the proffered bribe — one she'd subtly solicited from the poor fellow to look the other way as he broke the law.

"Damn, she's quick," Molly admired.

"Always have been," from behind, shimmery hair flouncing as we both turned, startled. "Seed money," doubtfully-Helena fanned the bills. "Courtesy the Société d'Exploitation de la Tour Eiffel," she flashed a lying name-tag.

"Exploitation is right." Not speaking French as I don't, it was the only word besides Eiffel I'd understood. Before I could say more, she stepped back and around sideways, appearing behind another hapless mark, tapping her shoulder as the woman fixed eye to the finder.

"Can you do that?" Molly's big eyes looked into mine. "The step and poof thing," she waggled her fingers.

"Not one of my tricks," I skirted — I could, once, but it wasn't *mine*. "Usually go by goat," I oddly recalled.

"You have a goat?" Molly's delight at the mention of a ruminant was palpable. "I thought you just had the T-bird."

"Lenny's a relatively new acquaintance — much more comfortable, less bouncy and flouncy — and only because he's such a shit gambler."

"Well that hardly seems fair, Mr. I-can-always-win," she shot me an accusatory glare.

"Didn't even have to cheat," I crossed my heart, all honest-like. "He's just that terrible."

"Who's terrible?" I-know-her-name's-not-Helena scared the bejeezus out of the both of us.

"You are," I glared. "Quit that."

"I want to meet the goat," Molly pouted, already over it, returning to the ruminant.

"Later," I promised. "What are you up to?" I hadn't followed along this side-track just to watch tourists get played.

"Educating the uninformed as to the particularities of French law in regards to copyrighted performances," she smugly affirmed, vanishing a wad of Euros in a flourish of her hand, "and the permits necessary for their photographic recording and dissemination."

"I meant," already exasperated, "what's the seed money for? And which tower are we selling?"

"Details," she dismissed. Guess I taught her that one, too. "What were you doing at Ruth's?" Ruth Bostic, I'd never gotten around to introducing her. She kept the books on a variety of things — hard numbers I can use. I'd wanted a few figures after the near-miss.

"Oh, you know," I hemmed, stopping just short of hawing. "Running some numbers with the Remembrancer, or I was about to..." I trailed off, giving Helena-interrupted a glare. "You?"

"Rent's due." Shit, that meant mine was due soon. Not now, but soon. Maybe I should set a reminder thingy like Molly always used.

"So why'd you pop in and out again as soon as you saw me? Why not just pay up?"

"Cause, chum," I-simply-refuse bounced, perking up the corners of her smile, "I don't have it." She swirled away to look for another mark — this one on the other side of the square.

She'd been there to buy time. Beg for it. But I got the feeling that wasn't all. It was never simple with her — taught her that, too.

Molly joined beside me, watching the con at work as I worked the problem. "What does she need us for then? She's raking."

"Cause," I hawed this time, "she needs more than cash, and I have an inkling of where to get it." More than an inkling. A headache.

"Ooooh," Molly delighted. "Time for a caper then?"

Veritably, she bounced with glee.

I groaned.

"Come on then," Helena-her-name-tag-lied pipped. How dare she? When you can't trust a handy-dandy name tag, there's something disastrously wrong. But at least she was tenacious in following the instructions I'd set forth in another life. Another name. Another face.

"Where?" Molly caught her stride, dress carefully hiked to the knee.

We were in a nameless back alley — which I called Stanchion for no reason other than it was tasty — between buildings where a door opened where none was.

"Here, of course," our guide flourished her hands. "The bowels of the Bennett Museum." Red-velvet jacket — procured with the seed money, along with the lying tag — rumpled slightly as she crouched to step... down? "Mind the drop," she called, vanishing into shadow.

Into a boiler room we went — much to Molly's delight — beneath the museum whose falsified name-tag had lied to us all the way through the sparse cones of light depending from the dim bulbs overhead and out behind a velvet rope.

No guards cleared their throats as we slipped over the velvet and out, unquestioned. No docent with an utterly scandalized scowl fixed upon their face chastised us either. I suppose if you're already *behind* the velvet ropes, they don't feel the need to keep you from crossing back.

Our target was in sight: back to us, white hair swept severely to the nape, staring at the art on the wall, two underlings flanking him.

Let's do this. I fixed my tie and loosened my back.

Out of habit, I clocked the blinking cameras in the corners of the room, fields of view overlapping. My neck itched. Not my style, but I wasn't leading this little caper.

The plan was simple, she'd said: get in, scam the mark, get out.

"You have a buyer for a tarot card you don't even have?" Molly had become fascinated by the craft of the silver-haired con artist. Game recognize game, after all.

"If I had it," big blue eyes blinked, "I wouldn't need to sell it, now would I?" As if it were blindingly obvious. The illogic astounded. "Now," she breezed on, "you — Molly, right? — I don't know you, but if you're with this guy, I figure you can handle a lil razzle-dazzle."

Molly crinkled her eyes in delight, not giving anything away. Good girl.

"And how do *you* know Felix, Helena?" She called her by that name, fixing her a little more as the moniker. Cementing the assumed identity I'd given her.

"He's my best student, of course." Molly sputtered a little gag as let's-call-her-something-else went on. "A little slow on the uptake, sometimes," she tutted, "but comes through in a pinch."

Molly shot me a look. "Usually does, yeah. Student, huh?"

"Oh yes, taught him everything he knows!"
How-about-Eileen didn't catch the eyebrow raise of doubt appended to Molly's question as she tucked things various and sundry into her red velvet coat — necessities for the caper, I presumed.

"At one point, sure," I hedged, doing a little coin-pass sleight of hand I'd learned for Molly's bright eyes. "I've learned a few tricks since," I winked as she stifled a giggle. And before.

Molly's face slipped back to neutral as nah-not-Jasmine flipped back with a smile. "You can thank me for not calling him Jake. Felix is much better," maybe-Margaret nodded with certitude.

"Jake?" Molly perplexed a bit, seeing how it fit.

"Was dead set on calling himself that when we took him in at the school," let's-try-Jasmine-again recalled. "Never told me his real name." Still no.

"Jake? Cringe," she gacked. Ouch. "School?" Curiosity piqued.

"What's wrong with Jake?" I tried to distract, but wasn't shiny enough.

"The Saffron School for Confidence, of course," Jessica-doesn't-work gleamed as she clapped her hands excitedly. "Felix hasn't told you?" Eyes large and ever-innocent shifted all blame to me. She was good at that.

"No," Molly followed the shift. "That, or his name."

I charmed a smile. "S'as much my name as any other." They're tough to fit right.

"Still doing the cryptic thing, huh?" Michelle-no-maybe-one-L? turned to Molly, blatantly ignoring my whimsy as she rifled through a rack of clothes. Gotta look the part.

What? It just feels so good. So *me*, whatever my name may be.

Molly made a noise somewhere between scoff and laugh and duh — her body language speaking volumes more. How does she do that? One single sound accompanying a tuck of the elbows, slight twist of her neck, shoulders drawing back as if she's about to launch into full oration, but stopping short at a hairball.

Maybe it's some sort of psychic connection like her thing with animals because not-Mary got it right away, shaking her head as she tossed me a generic tux.

"Well," the recruitment spiel started, holding up a dress for Molly to try, "the Saffron School is the premier educational institution for the time-honored art of relieving the undeserving of their excesses by various methods and means," it went on while fetching accessories.

"Molly's pretty adept at the game already," I chimed in from the side, checking the slinky shimmer of the cocktail dress handed her.

"Thank you," Molly brightened in the mirror. "Too much?"

"Looks great," I gawped. Just a little. "Maybe ging…" er, I'd been about to say, cutting short as Molly'd reflexively started reddening her hair. Shit. My head jerked around, seeing trouble coming.

Not in front of *her,* I panicked, shattering the mirror, distracting prying eyes and snapping Molly's focus mid-twist.

Leading the Saffron School as she did, she knew about the other side of the street, so to speak, but she didn't necessarily know I was from it, or lots of other things I'd rather she didn't question. Believe it or not, I *don't* like attracting attention to myself. It just finds me.

So a little ding to my luck didn't seem like much to keep some things secret.

Wrong.

Now that I thought about it, I could have used the bit of luck I'd lost right about then as we stood behind the bars closing off the museum wing — Molly in her sparkles and me in a monkey suit. I hate tuxes, always have. They were better now thanks to Eddie, no more fucking tails, but still…

Tangent, sorry.

That had gone wrong — for us anyway — as my teacher-slash-student led us straight into a trap. What the fuck was wrong with me lately? I tugged at my tie, loosening it as Hector monologued — typical villain style.

Yep, Hector — the less-than-charming devil I'd conned out of the Last Chance — looked a lot older, having lost the Lantern's light. Kinda grumpy, too. He'd been blathering about revenge or retribution — some such nonsense — while I paid no attention, instead reconstructing my whole fuckup.

First, I let my guard down. Gotten all riled up about the piano-fall, I didn't see the more subtle knife of a friend cutting close. Didn't see how she'd pulled me away from the Remembrancer before I could ask my question — flustered and flouncy in my face. Sweeping me right along into her scheme. I *taught* her that, damnit.

Second, I went along on a scheme I didn't plan. I didn't trust my gut — the itch at the back of my neck when I saw the cameras pinning me in place. I should have walked right then — cameras never blink.

Third, Molly.

I'd been paying too much attention to her. Watching her like a hawk looking for signs of slipping, signs of... you know. She'd been fine after the whole debacle with the ginger fairy, Dena, all my shit coming down on her. I just hadn't realized. Got all worked up about shit I didn't need to and lost sight of our situation.

It's funny. Too much trust here, not enough there. Misplaced, I suppose. Unsettled.

Molly looked just a little scared.

Hector was blathering some bullshit about skinning us alive and how we'd pay and just being super fucking *small.*

I guess a year ago I might have been scared, too. Or pretended to be, anyway. Why the hell was I scared of this insignificant, puffed up... *creature*? I chose not to know any better, I guess.

I mean, credit where credit's due. He had the vibe down pat — he didn't have the shadow anymore, but he still had the sadistic bent. You could see it in his eyes. The way he'd treated his underlings. His bearing as he casually turned to face us after the trap had sprung. The way he'd set Helena-I'd-Named-her cowering into the corner — just short of bowing and scraping. Side note: how the *hell* had he come to hold the School's note? I guess I should find out.

Another time. Resigned sigh.

I just wanted things to be quiet.

That's really all I've wanted. Instead, a headache.

"How much, Olya?" I-called-her-by-her-real-name-o,
cutting Hector off — ignoring him to direct the question
toward my student beyond museum security. They thought
it'd keep me in. Well, that it'd keep *Felix* in. "What do you
owe this two-bit shuckster? Nevermind, I'll go ask Ruth."
Her mouth dropped, struck speechless for only the second
time I knew of.

The key flew from her to my hand — the one I'd trusted
to her decades ago. The one she'd hidden at all costs,
preserving secrets best kept. The one no one else knew about
— I now reclaimed.

"Molly," she jumped. Was my voice that different? "Take the
cards." I waved the display cases open.

Seventy-eight cards from an original printing of the
Smith-Waite deck had been on display with the original
Tower illustration at the Bennett. Olya had tricked me with
it, causing my current crumble. That was number four,
unbeknownst to her — Dena's hand at work.

In my mind, the Magician's key turned, away in my room,
buying me precious moments with the memory of my
beloved. Carefully, I removed the delicate drawing, feeling
her spirit imbued in the aged ink.

Everything Dena ever drew by any name bore the indelible
presence of her soul. I glanced at Molly, now harboring a
piece of it in the spot she'd lost. Frozen in the moment I'd
stolen as I slipped the Tower into my private collection.

The clock ticked on, the moment gone. I turned to open a
door in nothing.

"Am I the nails or the knife?" I wanted to know. Olya's
mouth tried to work.

"The what?" Hector — his best vitriol spent sputtering
paltry intimidations — tried to butt his confused ass in,
outraged at being entirely ignored this entire time.

"Beat it," I glared — fire lit in my eyes as Molly was
distracted gathering the tarot deck, "while I allow." Feeling
the bloodlust roar in my soul, I watched the pitiful devil
shrink in on himself — cringing and cowering despite the
bars between us. They would not keep him safe from the
violence buried deep inside - violence that raged to be set
loose on this stain.

No.

I quashed it.

But not before reducing Hector to a piddling puddle
spreading on the floor.

Mustering her last ounce of resilience, Olya sparkled and
quipped: "Why the horseshoe, of course, Master," she
bowed. Spine straightening, she stepped back and blipped
out of sight. Key or no, she still had tricks that were her own.

"Well, that secret's out," I sighed, turning. "Let's be off, shall
we?" I hooked my arm out for the sparkly Molly to take,
guiding her through to nothing.

Who even am I anymore? I wondered to no one.

Smile! It Scares Them

MANY WONDROUS AND FEARSOME things hide behind a smile...

Like the beautiful one Molly flashed at me... I knew I was in trouble.

"Felix," she sparkled in the nothing. "Care to explain what's going on?"

"Not really." I tried for a winning smile. Guess it got lost in the dark. That's what I'll tell myself anyway.

"Too bad," she crossed her arms and distracted me with her hips, kicked out at an alluring angle in the clingy dress.

"You asked for adventure." This time I went for a suave double-back redirect. No dice.

Would have better luck with dice than trying to dodge Molly in this mood — same smile spread as when she blatantly lo-jacked the T-bird right to my face.

"Okay," I moped. "Fine." I really didn't want to, but Molly deserved more at this point. Still not used to that.

I stalled — kicking at trash in this back alley I'd brought us to; dipping a shiny-toed shoe in garbage-water fit neither for possums nor trash-pandas, watching it ripple the streetlights obscuring the stars; and engaged in general mental dissociation whilst Molly waited, hand now on impatient hip.

I felt the heavy key in my pocket — the key I'd retrieved from Olya-who-I-once-named-Helena. Felt the weight of the worlds within throw me off balance a bit, stepping on a crack. Great.

"Right now we're in one of the back alleys," I began. "Good place to lay low," I hoped.

She saluted, following it up with an eye roll. Captain Obvious, I guess?

"Secret shortcuts. Side entrances most places." I walked, raising my head to look around the brickworks stapled with downspouts and escapes. I grabbed a ladder, clattering it down to the broken pavers. "The accumulated mistakes and misalignments of man," I held out my hand.

Molly shot a look askance before taking it, shifting the sparkly dress to sequined pants — practical for climbing, plus they had 'pocketses' as she frequently emphasized with extra s's. Ones she tucked the tarot into, freeing hands to climb.

We rose higher into the darkness above the lights below, switching back again and again, climbing the urban bramble.

"It's a place to simply *be* if you've nowhere else to," I paused, pointing out into the dwindling lights. "Existence can be a rare thing."

I felt more than saw Molly's eyes land on me, growing concerned, before looking back down at how far we'd come, then up — trying in vain to see how far yet. "Maybe we should have taken your goat?"

"Hora doesn't like the city," I shook my head. "Besides, we're almost there." I took the lead this time.

"Hora? Is that your goat's name?"

"The time goat belongs to no one," I loved saying things like that, "not even me." I shuffled off to the side across a plank

I'd kicked out, having come to the landing I was looking for. "Couple of leprechauns made me his acquaintance a few lives ago."

Molly puzzled *that one* out in the dark as I checked behind, drawing up the improvised bridge in case something followed.

"What are you looking for?" Circuits tripped, she left it for another time — smart girl — pursuing another thought.

"Gargoyles." Not much else could find us this high. Not Hector. Not Olya — though I didn't think she'd come looking.

"No clue what I expected you to say, but 'gargoyles' wasn't on my list."

"Same." I hadn't expected to nearly have a piano dropped on me earlier either, but there it was.

"Moving on," Molly did. "How high are we? I didn't think skyscrapers had escapes like that."

"Not sure," I considered, tasting the air. "Haven't been here in a long time. And there are a couple in Chicago."

"Are we in Chicago, then?"

"Not as such, was just an example." I recalled my time in the Second City, trying to place this particular back alley — no, not Chicago. Bits, maybe. I heard the El rumbling along as the iron rattled. "Okay, maybe a little Chicago. Like I said," I waved my hand out over the chaos interrupted by flashes of forgotten sprawl winking in and out — in flux as things forgot and remembered, "accumulated side tracks. Lost directions."

Sounds warred in Molly's throat, fighting to see what got asked next. I could see the veritable cornucopia of questions burgeoning behind her eyes as they raced through the mysterious bits she'd gathered together.

"Important part is Hector *can't* get here." Obnoxious prick. "And Olya won't." Not now.

"You never told me you were kinky," she non-sequitured. *Quite the logic leap there, Molls,* I quirked my eyebrow. "Helena — you called her Olya? — called you 'Master,'" she added.

Ah. Complicated.

"Mind out of the gutter," I tisked with a slight wink. "I'm her teacher."

"But I thought..."

"She was mine? Yeah," I rubbed the back of my neck, "she's that, too. Look," I half-shrugged, waving my hands while my mouth tried to find the words — as if the motions explained the intricate complexities of the whole situation.

"That weird, huh," she saved me.

"Another life," I started. "Founded the Saffron School, set Olya up to run the thing," I flashed the key, "while I went hunting for chickens out west," I tied the threads together, "and to kinda protect some shit and have a fallback if things went..."

"As they went," Molly ventured.

"Anyway," I dodged the threatening memories — ever haunting my subconscious, "told her to call herself Helena, set a trigger, and Bob's your uncle."

"I don't think I have any uncles." Molly thought for a second, wry smile and glimmer of laughter lighting in her eyes. She knew how close to the edge she tread, walking it back a bit.

Chuckle. Does the soul good — tattered and piecemeal as they get.

Achoo.

God-fucking-damnit.

I nearly jumped over the side of the iron rail as Molly reflexively swung a haymaker at the source of the sneeze.

"Easy now," the sneezing man whoaed. Birdshit in his beard, he smiled through black teeth as he dipped and ducked, springing back upright in the afterglow of forgotten light. "Good golly Miss Molly, I meant no offense, I did."

People getting the drop on me left and right, damn. First Hector slyed his way into cornering me at the museum — triggering the alarm just as he slipped from the Tower trap, leaving us red-handed. Now the sneezing man — Ez B to his foes and friends, of which I was regrettably one — snuck right damn up behind me while I was all monologuey with Molly. Ruined a perfectly nice moment, too.

Maybe that was for the best, though. Still not ready.

"Fantastic," he gave no mind to the poorly aimed punch, "I see you're dressed for the ball." Ez B cocked his head and hunched a shoulder, reaching out to rub the dirty collar of my tux with his dirtier thumb.

It smelled like shit. Like he'd actually stuck it in a smoldering, steaming pile of feces, smeared it around, then covered the thumb in cling wrap just to preserve the fetid aroma for my personal enjoyment.

That was new. Hadn't had that last we talked, but Ez was ever looking for new ways to put people off. To test them. It was annoying, really.

"I'm not going," I dismissed, turning to look out over the back alleys spreading into the darkness. Sirens alarmed in the distance as I tried to quiet the bells in my own head. No fucking way I was going to the ball, not like this — I risked a glance over at Molly — too much to lose when I was so fucking far off my game.

"You've no choice but— " Achoo, he interrupted his own self.

"Bless you," Molly with the benediction. "What but? What *ball*?"

"Less ball, more trap to trip," I grumbled, having had my fill of traps.

"The Lunatic Ball, my lovely dove," Ez B smiled through his stained and broken teeth, wiping a bit of birdshit from his nose. Charming.

The sirens grew louder, less distant, as red glow filled the alley below. Needed to cut this short — Ez grew more there as we spoke.

"Yeah no," Molly agreed with me. "I think I'm alright, thanks."

"But it's by far the most magical event of the year," he tried more charm and less threat. "You'll meet the most fascinating figures ever to cut a rug — or wear one." Ez flipped his own hair back, revealing a balding and scarred pate. "You think you've seen it all? Wait until the Lunatic Ball."

Achoo.

"Fuck you," my benediction less kind.

He shot me a look, meaningful-like. "All *your* friends are coming, too."

The sirens stopped, alarming. Normally, I'd think that was a good thing — buuuuuut, typically it means they got where they were going. I shot to the edge, looking down at the whirling woos and flickering flashers.

My turn to grab the sneezing man's collar. "What've you done?"

Iron clamped my wrist in turn. "I? Nothing toward you," he pried one finger from his collar. "You, dear foe, stuck your head up." A second finger loosened. "And now they come for it."

I heard clattering boots on the urban bramble we'd climbed.

Clang. Clang. Rhythmic clang.

"Felix?"

One second, I didn't comfort. My head pounded, blood rushing, closing in as I ran through my list.

"*Who*'s coming?"

Crumble. From... above?

"FELIX!"

I'm not sure what happened next — one second Molly was screaming for me and the next, she's laughing her ass off with the slinky gargoyle who'd very likely tried to drop a piano on us just hours earlier.

Or its cousin. Hard to tell.

I mean — I was there for the strange sequence of events that led to us sitting on a cracked kitchen floor sharing a box of wine, sure, but even bearing witness to it...

Rewind.

Crackle, clatter, clang... all the sounds closing in on the scream.

Our new friend — wasn't at the time — Gregory, I've taken to calling him because our assailant neglected to wear a handy name tag. Right, Gregory sprung down from the shadows, eyes lit red and claws shkissing for blood. Mine.

Sparks flew as the gargoyle's strike sparked through the iron rail I'd leaned over to see the sirens flashing below, neatly severing three slices sent tumbling into the pools of red. Hissing, it turned where I'd stood until moments before — buried instinct saving my neck once more as it bubbled to the surface along with memories of...

A sword? Stabbed into the dirt of a glade, abandoned, vines twining the blade and hilt.

A voice in my head keened a thousand ways. My hand itched for the supple leather wrappings as it reflexively drew the sword not at my side — useless to parry the next swipe of the gargoyle's claws.

Shit. I cringed, expecting the pain that should follow the scything sickles.

"Where are your manners!?" Molly intercepted the frothing creature with the admonishing tone I'd so often heard used on wayward critters, stopping it cold and confused. "Shouting 'revenge,' 'blood enemy mine,' and," she paused momentarily, cocking her ear to better listens, "'kinslayer' is it?"

"Ba'lecry," the gargoyle sulked.

"Oh! A battle cry," Molly rolled her eyes, seeking patience. "A battle cry! If you set up an ambush, boy, that's not the time for a battle cry." True, someone'd been watching too much telly. Molly went on. "You face your foe head-on, then you get a battle cry! A cry for honor and dignity so the heavens hear your spirit. A cry for respect when injustice has been done and no other means of resolution appear." Such fervor. "The stone you were hewn from has more sense..." she muttered as the gargoyle stared. "Did no one teach you how to behave?"

Shock plastered across his misshapen face, slowly blending with shame until finally, his shoulders sank, deflated. All the anger and rage fled in the face of Molly's chastising.

"I asked you a question!" She actually cuffed the back of Gregory's head, reprimanding him like a spoiled child.

"No teach!" Gregory wailed, turning on me again. Hate radiated from his eyes like embers of a dying sun. "Your fault," his claws flexed. "Kinslayer." He tensed to leap.

"STOP. RIGHT. THERE." Molly clamped her slim hand on the gargoyle's shoulder — immovable as the bones of the earth, rooting the living stone in place. "You've a grievance and I'll hear you out. But we'll do this properly." Her eyes swept the iron landing, ensuring no one did anything stupid — specifically me, by unbidden reflex. "No shouting. No ambush," she paused, thinking, "and over something to drink."

Ez B chuckled from behind, bursting the taut bubble of breaths bated. "I see why Hank likes her," he said to me as I cleared the fog in my head.

"He has good taste," Molly chippered to the sneezing man before returning attention to the gargoyle, her hand never moving, emanating calm and peace. "I know you're upset. Shh," she comforted, "let's get this sorted, shall we?"

Her eyes traced up to mine — worry, doubt, a dozen questions unanswered danced in their clear depths.

Clang. Clang. Indistinct grumbles came from the ascending iron among clearer shouts of "Up there!" And "Get yer arse out my face, Higgens. Keep a move on!"

"Of course," I smiled at the indecipherable edifice of the gargoyle's face. It looked like a Gregory I once knew — hence, Gregory. The key burned in my pocket, aching to be used — petulant thing, at times. Probably drove poor Olya mad, I could feel. Another debt owed. I sighed and twisted the key in air, opening a crack of green exit light in the darkness. "Let's shall," I motioned through the portal most courteously.

Ez B spread a smile and hitched his pack higher with his shit-stank fingers as he leisurely strutted out from the back alley.

Next slinked Gregory — upon closer look, the gargoyle seemed shrunken and deformed as it sneered, tongue slightly slavering through a misshapen jaw. "Devilsavage," it garbled gruff.

Last came Molly, strained smile fixed in place. She didn't ease as she neared me like she had of late. Tension radiated from her too-stiff spine through her pinned-back shoulders, and clenched high in her rear as she stepped through the secret shortcut and into the discarded kitchen where we found boxes of wine.

"Now," Molly fixed me with her gaze. "Our new friend has some startlingly strong allegations, Felix." Fun. I deflated, turning the mug upright to drain the last drop of grown-up grape juice. Have I mentioned I'm not a huge wine fan? But when needs must, it does.

"They're probably true," I cut to the chase, "after a fashion, I suppose," I sighed. "Remember how I used to not be a nice guy?" I'd hoped we'd have our juice boxes and skip this part.

Ez B laughed, muttering: "Fiendish flaming hellspawn more like," behind his own mug. Boiling blood-hiss echoed in his words.

"So you wrote," Molly nodded. "But that was a different you, yes?" She nodded, emphasizing this to Gregory. "You, Felix Chance, didn't kill his family, right?" She looked sick. Broken shells in a sacked rookery came flashing to mind. Fetid goo and half-formed... well, it wasn't pretty.

"My hands will never be clean," I admitted, "but no, I'm not him," I prayed, "that me was wiped away in the waters of Lethe." Until it wasn't, I didn't add. "Dead as any me can be," instead — half-true.

The stains of my past will never let me be.

...

..

.

"Where do you think you're going, mister?" Molly propped a hand on sparkling hip.

Without thinking, I'd moved to the break in the floor of the bombed-out building — the key really reflected one's mentality, I recalled. Spooky. I'd felt the bridge burning with my admission and my subconscious acted on it. Coward.

One thing bugged me though, swimming up through the wine-addle.

"How'd..." I gestured toward Gregory, not having named him aloud... "find me?" No one should know this face. Even St Germain hadn't. Another debt.

"I can answer that one, dear foe," Ez B with the hurtful words. I'd thought we were on... well... not *bad* terms. "It's actually why I've been trying to get your damn attention."

Achoo.

"Gesundheit," the gargoyle ground the blessing.

"Yeah well," prevarication suits me, "I wasn't in the mood."

"And as such you nearly had your ivories tickled by Gregory here, as I believe you've been calling them," the sneezing man tapped his temple.

How? No, focus.

"That was you?" Molly pulled away, weaving under the wine. Pointed finger accusing.

"Sorry," Gregory shrank. "Mad." A monster of few words, our Gregory — at least aloud. I imagine Molly got a fuller picture of the situation, complete with layers of emotion and context. "Hit."

"And to that point," Ez B interjected. "You've a price on your head..."

"I'm aware," I started to interrupt when Ez returned the favor.

"No, now-*you*, Felix Chance," he got in my face, bopping my forehead, "has a price on his head."

"Nonsense," I phahed, borrowing one from Hank. "None of *them* knows this face and that are connected." Only the trusted and the dead.

"They do now, courtesy one surly and cussed goblin."

Goddamnit Bill.

"He's been talkin'."

Get out of my head, I thought. The sneezing man crinkled his eyes, seeing far too much — those hadn't been gimmes.

"He couldn't just keep his mouth shut and wait?" I grumbled aloud just to shift focus from the prying thoughts.

"Oh he's been waiting, dear foe." Again with that? "And took that punting you gave him amiss. Final straw and all that." Damn, he knew a lot. "I was sent to warn you such, and in your infinite wisdom, you deigned to ignore that missive."

"What's with the foe thing?" Molly with the assist. "Are you after him, too?"

"Oh no, I just like stirring the shit," he circled a stained finger my way. "So to speak."

"Like we don't have enough of that." True, girl, true. I opened more wine to shut everyone up and think.

"They're coming, you meant..." I'd been drinking through the long list in my head as the box emptied.

"Yes." Ez hiccuped, letting it breathe. "*All* of them. Probably."

"Probably?"

"Some might not be. I lost count," Ez breezed. "Not my job." True, needed to double back and see Aunty Ruth since we were so rudely interrupted.

Well, at least that explains why did-I-call-her-Helena pounced on me — she didn't know the backstory, just the fee I'd fetch. And why Hector'd showed up. Two birds, one stone for him — getting a payday for your personal vendetta is always nice.

"Why *is* everyone after you, Felix?" Molly in her cups. I couldn't let my shit splash on her.

"There's a different me living in the head of everyone I meet," I said, eyes flashing toward Gregory. "Some of me are the villain of the story."

Silence. Guilt pangs stabbed as Molly bit her lip, thinking. At times, I'm not even sure what I am in my own story.

"Spilt milk and all that," I waved it off. Nothing doing, only way out is through. "Guess I better go see a countant," I flipped the key through my fingers, feeling for the door to the burlesque we'd left.

"She's not there," Ez butted in.

Seriously stop that.

"She'll be at the ball."

Great. I guess I did have to go, after all.

"You're not a bad guy in my story," Molly, out of nowhere.

She hadn't said much since the wine ran out. Too much to think about. Reticence reigned as we readied for the ball — twisting to fix tuxes and dresses, better than any dry cleaner. Wordless motions conveyed all necessary meaning.

She'd remained silent even as we walked through endless midnight to reach the ball, our steps guided by the sole light of a flickering candle pointing the way in sparks and sputters — growing stronger as we neared and waning if we mis-turned in an unlit sky.

"I wanted to tell you before," she gestured ahead of us.

The wayfinding candle was a cosmic game of hot-or-cold, basically, and now it blazed bright as curtains appeared to part in the darkness. Velvet, blacker than the night surrounding us, gave way to glittering gold and the clattering clink of too many glasses toasting our arrival.

"I know." I glanced to the side to see Molly's eyes alight like a cat's seeing its first Christmas tree. I wonder if that's why animals like her so much. Stop. Stray thoughts can get you killed.

"Are you sure this is a good idea?" Molly paused, adjusting her mask. The wonder and delight had melted away almost instantly, replaced by doubt.

"Terrible idea," I smiled and handed a white glove our calling card. "The absolute worst, but that's why it'll work." I winked through my own mask, holding out my hand for her to take.

Reluctantly she did, her face devoid of confidence — in me? Herself? Where had this temerity taken root? This was highly un-Molly. I brushed her cheek gently. "It's like any other con," I grinned, gripping her hand.

"The lady Brianna Wintergale," announced the herald, doing the lying for me. "And escort." That was me.

"Smile," I whispered as we stepped forward into the spotlight, "it scares them." A wicked glint caught in her eye as a very Molly smile spread. These fuckers were in for a shock.

Striding forward, our eyes caught the minglers in their milieu, looking down on those around them over their champagne flutes brimmed with bubbles. Glitter fluttered in the air, iridescent in the flames of the gathered candles floating aimless now that the ways had been found.

One mote fluttered too close, catching aflame with a scream and falling to ash. I felt Molly's nails dig slightly in at the shock and startle, quickly recovering her composure. From the ash fluttered aloft a gossamer moth, circling yet another candle too closely.

"Phoenix moths," I warned. "Don't touch."

"Pretty," disconcerting, she didn't add, though I felt she wanted to.

Through the crowd we waltzed, making our faked presence known. The masks gave off an aura of other, obscuring the wearers — to our benefit as well — but they were not perfect by any stretch and reality bled through, giving glimpse to hidden horrors and wonders tenfold.

The Lunatic Ball — a glitzy place for those of every stripe and creed to gather and cavort. Gods and monsters, folk fair and foul, beings mundane and less-so — I spotted several familiar to myselves past and present shining through the gaps. Several more I did not know, now nor then, to my recollection — some appearing as ordinary people do. Lost perhaps? Their way mislaid? A fevered dream of a goblin

king, most like, burst and gone again once they woke. All set
to celebrate the missing moon — lucky number thirteen.

I didn't recall it being this popular before — generally
attended by the *mostly* mundane, at least those with higher
aspirations — but who knew? I'd been out of circulation
for a while. From the looks of things, it seemed the higher
realms finally deigned to attend. Maybe they got bored?

Or, like anything with them, it takes a few centuries to catch
their eye — stupid an idea as that is. I was just glad to see
at least one friendly face amongst the eldritch bunch as I
scanned for more. I nodded toward the pink feather boa-clad
figure — shorter than I'm used to seeing him — who nodded
back, peacock feathers dallying around his head as he did
— already they seemed dillied out. As much as I wanted
to bee-line for the familiar, I restrained myself lest my shit
splash him too.

"Shall we dance?" I held a hand for Molly to take. It's
important — no matter what situation you're in — to take
a step back, breathe, and savor the moment.

And in this moment, she looked stunning. Flowering gold
picked over black cascaded down to barely brush the
polished marble floor over which she did glide. Gawkward
girl I'd met a lifetime ago — only a year or so? Still a lifetime
— gone. Ripped jeans and Bigfoot tee a mere memory folded
into the elegant woman I escorted to the dance floor. My
heartbeat stilled as she echoed my Dena once more.

I breathed, setting aside the confusion for now and simply
losing myself in a moment that could always be my last.

We danced. Magical rhythms flowing through feet I'd not
remembered — nor could I tell you exactly what I'd done.
Cheese is cheese, dance is dance. The experience is the
important part — we'd simply moved as one for the moment.
United.

She exhaled, her flush face close to mine — the spell broke
as eyes pried between us. I'd not noticed the room fall silent

as we'd had our breathless moment. I felt her tense against me as she, too, noticed the predatory eyes upon us.

"Everyone's staring," she whispered.

"Of course," I smiled. "You're rather ravishing," I distracted with a flirt. Down boy. *This is Molly*, I reminded myself, guiding her from the dance floor.

"I don't think we want *this* crowd staring," she sobered, shedding the heady feeling she'd had dancing, "now do we?"

"Don't worry about it." I wove her through the predators gathered. Eying each and every one as we passed.

"I think it's a little worrisome being trapped in here with them," she smiled tensely.

"Don't think of it like that." I locked eyes with her. "*They're* the ones trapped," I grinned my toothiest. "With *us*." I gave a big show of laughter as I patted her hand hooked over my arm, marching straight for our friend.

Never show weakness.

"Girl, you are simply smashing," a familiar voice rumbled from above the pink boa. A shorter Sassy took Molly's hand for a twirl — the mask rendering his height slightly less, but still obvious.

"Sassy!" she gleed, jumping for his neck. "What're you doing here? Why're you..." She gestured at his apparent lack of height.

The dull roar resumed around us as our spectacle receded in favor of others. On the floor currently, unless I missed my guess, was the Erlking and his latest tart. My face puckered, looking aside to Sassy to see his reaction.

"And just *who* are you wearing?" Sassy ignored the commotion, returning to Molly. "It's fab," he felt the fabric.

"Moi," Molly giggled, having twisted herself into the fancy threads — she'd gotten *good* at that.

"I'm surprised you didn't go for something more," he waved his hand, thinking, "backless," Sassy settled on, "and velvet." He felt invisible material between his fingers as he sought more words.

"Don't expose your back to a threat," Molly simply said — the rationale for her clinging cloth armor laid bare. A black silken cape unfurled, further illustrating her point.

"Fair." Sassy cocked his head, fluffing his boa.

"Souvenir photo?" A glimp popped up from the edge of the crowd — part goblin part imp — wielding an old flashbulb camera. The kind in the movies — big wooden handle, giant popper up top. "Remember your precious moments," it flittered up to their eyeline.

I wanted no part of this — no photos, please — sidling to the side as Sassy and Molly squared up with a grinning "Sure!" as they struck a pose.

The bulb blinded — brilliant white light dazzling the eyes as stars swam through time. The glimp counted ten before peeling paper off the camera back, ripping and shaking it as it stiffened — a frame of sorts grew from the edges of the memento to finish it off. The creature made a squinty face, tongue sticking out as it flickered between the photo and the pair within — an artiste admiring their handiwork — before handing the now rigid photo-in-frame to Molly.

Besties as they were, they pored over the photo all giddy, pointing out how great each other looked as the glimp turned to me, white glove held high. "One silver second, do you please?"

I suppressed the goggling my eyes desired, controlling my impulse to haggle and deride the glimp as a rip-off. *A whole second? Outrageous!* Instead, my practiced hand flourished to reveal a shining silver coin stamped with a clock.

A second for Molly was worth it, I reminded as I parted with the fleeting time — the glimp flittering off to another mark.

"That was two months ago!" What was? I turned attention back to the fawning pair. "At the shoe place." Thank you, Molly.

"May I see?" I held out my hand for the memory frame, suspicious. Molly's face filled with confusion, looking between the picture, Sassy, and myself.

The frame did indeed contain a shot of Molly and Sassy-pants shoe shopping — at Orym and Dain's swanky new digs, their work all the rage in fashion — which switched to one of them at Beckett's singing karaoke. A couple more slides faded in and out of frame before circling back to tonight's festivities.

"More than just a memento of tonight, I see." I liked it not.

"That's so cool!" Molly snatched the slideshow back, ignoring the veiled threat it posed.

"Sure is sweetheart," Sassy smiled. "And girl, you slay," he squeed a bit for positivity's sake, picking up what was put down. "But damn! Couldn't they have used higher angles on me," he yeeshed.

"Love," Molly put her hand on Sassy's arm gently, "you're nearly three times anyone's height. Ain't no one got a selfie stick that long."

"I'll use a tree, thank you very much," Sassy flipped his head back — his tone bursting Molly into laughter.

"That was a great day," Molly turned attention back to the scrolling memories, now on the shoe store. "I hope Dain's doing better, seemed a might frail."

"Not so good, last I heard," Sassy shook his head, "only ate fifty-three cents the other week. All skin and bones. Orym's taking it rough." Sad. The cobbler *was* getting up there, near three hundred, I'd guess. Maybe I should pop by with a bit of gold.

On to other topics as I'd reminisced, Sassy dishing the dirt for Molly — bringing her up to speed on the current tea of the attendees.

"Erl there," Sassy leaned in, pointing to the masked Erlking sporting a frizzy fro behind the mask where his antlers should go. "He's got a tattoo of himself," he started.

"That's not so bad," Molly interrupted.

Sassy-pants pulled a face. "Over his dick," his brows waggled as Molly's eyes went wide.

"Girl, it gets better," he oohed. "He's in full armor," he paused, curling his hand down low, "jousting." He thrust for affect.

More than I ever wanted to know, and still, they went on.

"*And* there were certainly some questions of where she picked up that glitter she gave him..." I tuned out and walked off at that — not caring who gave who what venereal disease.

"A one Knight stand," Molly with the zinger, sending them both into gigglefits.

On that note, I needed some air.

"Oh, lump it," a frustrated fellow spat as I exited the gaiety of the gala. "Dear boy," I suppressed a wince, "do you have a light? I'm near to risking a brush with a fallen Phoenix here."

"Sure," I fished around for show — twisting a memento into my hand during the distraction. "Just a... aha!" I produced the striking rod St Germain had made for me in another lie as the slender fellow stepped closer — the smooth cylinder felt slick in my hand as I twiddled it between my fingers.

"You're a veritable lifesaver and a saint." Smartly snapping a cane beneath one arm — obviously ornamental, the fellow reeked of popinjay even amongst the glitz and glam of the ball — this ginger presented a rolled leaf for lighting.

Yep, a ginger. I felt a momentary pang of jealousy at the hair aflame like rubies in a dying fire — I'd always wanted to be a ginger. Never had *that* particular stroke of luck, even with all the new faces manifest. Sure, I could fake it in a twist — or even via mundane means — but it just wouldn't be the same. There's something special coming upon it honest.

With a flourish, I cracked the rod in half along the cleverly hidden seam, striking the naphtha match to violet light.

"Curious lighter." The fellow drew on the cigarette — the smoke curling from the thin tip smelled exotic, of berries and spice. Looked it, too, being red and all. Not like the starkly ginger hair I pined for, nor the red of blood. A sort of pinkly red verging on the fluoresce — excited by the alchemic light.

"Curious smoke," I countered, flicking the memento mori closed and disappearing it inside my jacket. Flame sealed once more, the smoke took a more pastel stance.

"Bidis." Rose petal clouds drifted further in the air, swirling and sworling in nearly hypnotic patterns. "They're a bit heavy dewy..."

"Heavy *dewy*," I interrupted, eyebrow raised.

"Heavy de-ew-ty," he enunciated. "Drop me t's sometimes like that. Illegal most places now, I'm afraid," he went on. "Tasty, though. Drag?"

"Pass, minus the puff," I cracked wise. "Never my thing. Thanks, though." Only polite.

"So why the strike of naphtha?" Curious eyes met mine, sparking distant knowledge. "Unless I miss my guess — which I don't — rather distinctive smell."

"Neither flammable nor inflammable is it," I cribbed the Count's line. "Memory of a friend. He liked his smokes."

"Most alchemists do," the stranger dropped all nonchalant, pricking my guard.

"Who said he was an alchemist?"

"You did, obviously." I was totally lost. "Snap out of it, *dear boy*." Now this ginger was deliberately goading me with a grin, preening for my benefit. I've heard some are indeed evil. Perhaps this was one, or perhaps...

I peered close. It couldn't be... could it? He'd been immortal...

Tall and slender. Check. Flamboyant, certainly. No diamond. Strike. But he'd used it up for Molly. Far too colorful to be...

"No," the preening fellow denied. "I'm not him, nor have I ever been or taken any name close to his."

"Then who are you?" Another alchemist came to mind, darkly, but that chicken had been plucked.

"I am who I am, no yams to be seen," he punned. "But you may call me Fulcanelli," he swept, arm arcing smoke wide, "the Last Alchemist, by dismal sobriquet. A student of the late St Germain."

"So you've a temper, do you?" Leaping logic — ignore the stab of memory — the ginger made sense now. Little volcano.

"Every meaning of the word," the Last Alchemist smiled. "Yes. Forged of a soul in the great work."

That was saying something. I never knew the deeper mysteries of the Count's trade — only bits and pieces I'd observed or what little he'd actually taught me. Like making gold — handy trick there.

"He never mentioned you," I tested his temper with a prick.

"You were on the outs by my time." Fulcanelli's face pinched, eyes stabbing at me. "That pained him greatly, you ungrateful little shit."

"Now see…" I stopped. *He* was testing *me*.

"I see many things you do not," he carried on. "Including the sad state you are in, *dear boy*," laced with venom and mockery.

"Can you not?" I suppressed the blinding rage so easy to draw of late, clenching my fist. "My name is Felix."

"Now it is, as you say," the smoke from his cigarette laced his words. "But your three-pence name is not your truth."

"Is anything?" I slipped from rage to sly, deflecting.

"You don't even know yourself, anymore," the character assault continued.

"Kind of the point." I'd run.

"You're in shambles," he ignored, waving his smoke all over. "Pathetic mewling shadow of what was once…" he trailed. "Not worth his life." His pronouncement, definitive.

Silence hung, dancing in the air between us with the wafting rose plume. It was the truth threatening to break me that very moment — the new guilt plaguing my list of sins. I would not break — could not break.

"Better," he pronounced at last — eyes flickering about me as I stood, jaw clenched. "I begin to see a glimmer of what he was talking about."

Which was?

"You're going to need it, I'm afraid," he didn't answer.

From inside, the band struck a whimsical tune, signaling a change.

The Phantasmagoria had begun.

"Guess that's our cue... and I'm talking to myself," I told myself.

My opinionated — fuck it, asshole — companion vanished by the time my eyes traveled from the open doors back to where he'd stood.

"So much for some fresh air," I continued talking to myself, given my lack of company — no one to talk to means no one to call you crazy, either. The ones left on the inside, though, they were batshit.

Case in point, the chanting.

"We remember," the crowd began as I passed back in.

"*We remember.*

"*We remember the month stolen from our eyes.*

"*We remember.*

"*We remember the moon stolen from our skies.*

"Here! Come cross the lumiere, twist of shadow and light," a masked figure in a tailed coat flourished as the lights dipped.

The floating candles snuffed out one by one, drawing the remaining Phoenix moths along the room — colliding and combusting in a cascade of flame that focused into a single source in the middle of the ball.

The roiling ball of light cast shadows that danced across the air — forming figures from the story yet to be told.

I slipped back in amongst the rapt crowd, looking for Molly and Sassy-pants as the story of the stolen moon unfolded in the chiaroscuro of the phantasmagoria.

Like any journey it began with a fool, all innocent and new — unwary, as fools tend to be, but rife with possibilities. The infinite spread before them as they toed the edge of the cliff.

The shadows moved, transfiguring into forms best left forgotten — not that they'd ever let me. Kings and queens, empires that rise and fall like the sun and stars, crumbling away as had the tower now in my collection — all intertwined to tell of the lost moon.

"We remember.

"We remember the tides drawn through your haze.

"We remember.

"We remember the nights spent safe in your gaze.

The showman bowed his head in solemnity, drawing all to silence.

"We remember." He raised his head again, taking in the crowd with a sweeping finger. "We remember! Yes we do!" Fired up like a preacher taken by the Holy Spirit.

Tears filled his eyes as he carried on the act.

"What do they remember?" Molly with the aside to Sassy.

"Nothing really," I startled Molly. "Can't remember things that never happened. All just propaganda now."

"What does a goose in a tophat have to do with anything?" Molly cocked a hand on hip, face set with a wry smile.

"Also nothing," I laughed, "but I like your version better." Much better than what'd actually happened on the moonless night that followed all... *that mess.*

"Did you find who you were looking for?" Molly knew me too well.

"Nope," and it was disconcerting. "Found lots of people I *wasn't* looking for, though." Luckily, only the one had spotted me.

The one who rode up in the midst of the crowd just then upon a gilded cloud. Pretty audacious entrance, if you ask me. But points for style.

"We remember," Fulcanelli began.

The moon slain to grant the Dawn power, I finished to myself. I was getting sick of the pomp and hated everything the Golden Dawn had become. And I was getting pissed I hadn't found Ruth like Ez'd said I should — I'd only put up with this self-aggrandizing sycophantry to see her again.

"Hello sweetie," my favorite aunty said, perhaps summoned by my thought. "What a surprise to find you here."

Delighted, I turned to see her resplendent in her silver mask. "How could I miss it?"

"Lots of ways," she laughed. "I wouldn't be here if I wasn't working." Her laugh turned down for the briefest moment — a crack in the ever-cheery demeanor. She liked these fools about as much as I did, it seemed.

"About that," I hedged, wracking my brain for an out. A stall tactic. A point for smooth-talking negotiation. I'd thought I had a plan — or at least would come up with one — to work something out...

"That's why I'm here, sweetie." The remembrancer had come to collect. Gentle and sweet as Ruth seemed, she collected every debt ever owed — and I was coming up short. "We need to settle up," she smiled.

A Book Unwritten

"SO," I SAID, KINDA awkward. "You're a dragon, huh?"

Elliot rubbed his head against my hand, ignoring the commentary.

"Seems like something I ought to have known," I mused aloud — not like I could talk to animals. That was Molly's thing.

The tail flick that earned spoke volumes. If he'd wanted me to know, I guess I'd have known.

"Or that you can talk," I carried on, feline fickleness be damned. And not talk in the Molly way. I'd heard him at the ball.

"Thanks, by the way." He'd really saved my bacon with Ruth. "I'd say I owe you, but I know that's exactly why you did it." The smug look on his face as he rolled to request belly scratches sealed it. Clever dragon.

"Hey, if that's all you want for spotting my rent." I gave the good scratches — fingernails and circular rubs. Just don't touch my face. Apparently this one was allergic to cats — dragon-cats included. They must not be hypo-allergenic, strange for a shifter — or maybe I was allergic to dragons. That one's not included on standard allergy panels.

Out came the claws. "Ow!" I figured time for scratches was over as Elliot gave me the imperious 'How dare you?' stare. Dragon-cats, am I right?

I pulled back the gashed arm — careful to let the claws disengage — before he decided to bite for good measure. At least he didn't hurk a fireball at me.

"Someone's in a mood."

"He's always in a mood," Marty, from the door. "Decades now." He shelved a book, shortening his lifespan. "Mood."

"Marty," I started. "How long've you been his familiar?" I'd have pegged it the other way around, myself. But stranger things. Even when I know, I don't know *everything*.

"This book smells funny," he dodged the question, pulling out a first edition of *The Bell Jar* for Elliot to inspect. Lifespan again added — constant flux, Marty's years, so long as he has books yet to shelve.

"Funny's not the word I'd use," I joked. "Not Sylvia's style. Good student, though. Sharp." Tangent for another time.

Over his readers, Marty shot me a look he'd probably learned from the cat. I wondered what else he'd learned from the draconian feline.

He was right, though. The book smelt peculiar. Almonds, a bit of vanilla — cookies, maybe? — and burned peanuts. Smoke damage wasn't uncommon for tomes that old. Must and mold as well. But malodorous defects such as those were isolated lest they infect the others.

The almond and vanilla cookie smells were unique. Same for the peanuts.

"Not again." The deep, raspy voice belonged not to Marty, rather to Elliot. "Damn imps infested my hoard, thus necessitating your aid."

He'd said something about my aid at the party, too.

Just about the time Ruth had come to collect, the ginger cat had wandered up, flicking tail back and forth slightly hypnotic.

"What are you doing here, Elliot?" Molly squeed and swooped, scooping the furry dragon up in her arms — totally seeming to forget the flambé part as she snuggled the fur. *Anything with fur,* I sighed to myself. I was suddenly reminded of the 'Here kitty kitty' meme.

For his part, Elliot didn't protest as Molly squeezed him close.

"Elliot?" Sassy quirked a brow, dubiously fluffing his ruffled boa – a bit discomfited. "That's…"

Before he could finish, the dragon-cat hissed, subtle smoke curling up through his whiskers. Maybe they had history. Wasn't getting involved — had enough of my own to deal with.

"Girl, I hope you know you're snuggling death," was all he said before butting the hell out.

"Hello Elliot," Ruth scratched the fluffy death in Molly's arms. "And how are you, precious?"

"I am well, Madame Remembrancer, save for slight troubles for which I need this one's aid," he leapt from Molly's arms to my shoulder, speaking for the first time.

"Hmm," she weighed us both with her eyes. "His book is long worn and many debts come due," she shifted to me. "Can you spare enough luck for one shod horse? No," she read my face. "Ill time for that."

"A forbearance, perhaps?" I quickly offered in the opening. "I can offer collateral for your keeping until I retrieve the *other*." I didn't want to, but pulled the Tower from the twist.

"And I shall guarantee his repayment," Elliot weighed in — actually growing heavier at the words.

"Oh, that's lovely," Ruth gushed at the imbued illustration, slipping on spectacles — her appraising eyes saw deeply its value. "Yes, that will do nicely."

"Until I pay the debts owed," I reiterated, loath to let go of any piece done by Dena's hand.

"It shall be safe with me, sweetie," she smiled genuine warmth, temporarily square. "Until your debts are paid," she agreed, slipping it into her handbag. Who knew what riches *that* held. Whenever I'd paid the rent before, she slipped it into her bag. Sometimes it was white leather Louis Vuitton. Others Gucci, Prada, and a bunch I had no clue what they were, being less brand apparent — just that they were stupidly expensive. "Now, if you'll excuse me, I've a few other collections to make," she tsked.

My question!

"If you've a second..." I started.

"Of course, sweetie," she laughed. "What is it?" Again, full earnest attention. I took a deep breath.

"How many ways?" If I know, I can tweak the odds.

She thought for a second, running her finger down an invisible page.

"Ultimately," she looked up at me, concern in her eyes, "one."

One. Shit.

"One," Molly echoed from the edge, "there's only one way out?"

"Oh," the tallier started, "there are lots of ways to go, turns to take. Seven, then three," she flipped through the read ledger, "oh, nineteen here," she smiled kindly over her glasses.

"That's more like it," Molly nodded, knowing the more straws I had to grasp at, the better. Nineteen wasn't a lot, whatever kindly optimistic sound she made — normally there were thousands, even if a knife was pointed right at my throat.

"Sure, but," she took her glasses off and shut the mimicked book, "they dwindle. Six down to three and, finally," she held up an ominous finger, "one."

Molly frowned. "I guess one is better than none," she flipped to cheer.

"Yeah," I half smiled, trying not to let on.

There's always one, no matter what. It's just never pleasant.

"Totally *not* my fault." I thought. I wasn't terribly sure as this one was new, even for me.

"I'm no less suspicious," Molly eyed me sideways. Precariously balanced over a pit of doom as she was, it was an impressive feat — I'd have totally been watching mine. Feet, two e's.

"You're cheating," I snickered, seeing roots growing through her shoes.

"I don't want to hear that from *you*, of all people," she giggled with a charming side-eye. Fair. I did cheat. A lot. But it was always warranted. Used only in times of greatest need.

Or when I was bored — which was not the case this go round. Said pit of doom was quite fascinating. I've seen all sorts — traps with crocodiles snapping and splashing at the bottom, the kind where vipers got their name — *not* because of the extra little smell receptors as fuddy-duddy, lab-locked herpetologists would have you believe — and your classic spike-and-overgrown-vine — which are easily enough defeated by proper agility and grip strength.

This pit in particular had an alchemist's bent to it. Judging by the dust and debris that burst into flames as it fell through the cracks, this trap seemed to be filled with invisible fire.

"The pit full of protium phlogiston *isn't* your fault?" Doubt was all over her face. She was learning.

"It *could* be tritium," I lined the silver. Protium was bad enough. St Germain had loved the stuff — especially after he'd encountered it in Jabir's maze back in... another story, another time.

"What's that do?"

"Nagasaki," another voice pitched in — slightly inaccurate, but it got the point across. "Hiroshima. Simply horrible what a couple extra neutrons can do in the uranium pits." Fulcanelli joined the conversation from the side — leisurely dangling one leg from the ledge as he leaned against a broom. "Tried to warn those fools, but Oppy wouldn't listen." The last alchemist sighed a tad extravagantly. Might go so far as to say grandiloquent, if I wasn't doing my best impression of a mountain goat right then.

Hora would be proud. The pit wall — formerly the floor on which we'd walked — was sloped a manageable sixty-five degrees in its new orientation. While the time goat would have handled walking along an eighty-nine-degree slope just fine, I was proud I'd managed to balance passably on the nearly vertical floor.

"Well this isn't a uranium pit or a plutonium pit, thankfully," I countered once I'd balanced — totally different kind of pit. "Just a regular old pit trap in a dusty old passage in a nearly forgotten lair set up by someone who didn't want to be interrupted."

"Maybe we should have knocked," Molly hedged, her roots growing and shifting, carrying her feet surely to the other side. "To be polite."

"Manners maketh." Fulcanelli popped up, snapping the dust that had gathered on otherwise immaculate duds clear into the cleansing flame where it lit in azure delight — save for one spot.

One step then two, the alchemist strode onto air — invisible nothing holding firm under dust and polished shoes alike. Before each step, Fulcanelli swept the dust forward a little more, giving shape to the path.

"Someone's watched too many movies," Molly sighed from her rooted perch. Unflappable now, coming into her own, the Trenynn had taken the appearance of yet another immortal in stride when they'd turned up unannounced as this one had before our little expedition.

"Don't you have, like, a bar to run or something?" I'd tried to keep her from coming. I don't particularly like raiding old school lairs — and I do mean *old* — especially ones that possibly belong to an alchemist. Nasty surprises. Lost a face or two to some of the *security measures* and done some things I'd rather not speak of in others, I newly recalled.

"Hank's keeping an eye on it." Dismissive, carrying over to bold. "You trying to get rid of me or something?" Lips pursed as an eyebrow arched.

"No," I lied, busying myself about the kitchen packing snacks, bumping over the salt. Surreptitiously, I tossed it in the devil's eye.

"You ready?" Fulcanelli poked a head out of the closet — both of the broom variety — before appearing fully festooned in the finest adventurer's garb from a century prior.

"I'm definitely coming with you now," she crossed her arms, arching one eyebrow as a hip cocked out. "What's with the broom?"

"So much for NASA," I grumbled, making my way along the newly perpendicular floor.

"What's NASA got to do with this?" Molly's roots crept her forward, seeking new purchase amongst the crumbling stones.

"The broom," I continued the remembered inquiry. "NASA used to walk the halls with brooms held in front of them to find hydrogen fires early in the space age — as opposed to finding them with their face."

"Rocket fuel leaks," Fulcanelli confirmed, shoving the broom into the phlogiston pit to demonstrate. "Postmodern problems require primitive solutions." The straw bristles caught alight slightly higher than the dust. Not good. The flames were rising — damn science.

"Should probably get a move on." I chanced a hop, grabbing hold of a brick stuck too far out. Could've been a trap — so obvious — but it somehow wasn't. Didn't stop it from crumbling as I clutched though, my feet finding no purchase.

I fell. Molly gasped. Fulcanelli smirked. Son of a bitch.

Time didn't really slow, but I felt every second of gravity's nine-point-eight meters. Wasn't enough time for my life to start flashing before my eyes — really, I'd never get the whole reel in, but maybe some recent highlights would be nice.

Thoughts fluttered like blue butterflies across my mind as I felt the phlogiston kiss my feet — and stop. Replaced instead by Molly's screams as the roots she sent to save my soles caught alight instead.

Blue licked over the pulpy new growth, charring it with every scream. I jumped, springing off the platform growing from the rock, managing to reach the ledge on which the last alchemist stood watch.

"I'm clear, prune 'em," I frantically sought her eyes. Screwed shut against the pain, she couldn't see me. Couldn't hear me.

She burned, flame hungrily seeking rich new fuel.

They'd tried to burn Dena, too — witch that she wasn't. They'd burned so many innocents for naught but baseless fervor and fear — or jealousy. Fire to cleanse their souls as they were sent to their final judgment. So much bullshit.

I gripped the hilt at my hip. I would end this. I'd...

...the world went white with rage.

"Felix?" I felt Dena in my arms. Curled again against my chest, raven hair cascading down... no. She'd never called me *Felix*; that wasn't my name.

Not then.

"Felix!" Frightened. Bewildered. I focused on the green eyes staring into mine — shimmering with summer gold.

"Molly?" Where was I? What'd I done? No, I didn't care. She was safe, that's all that mattered — the spark of my wife growing dormant once more.

My life's full of blank spots, what's one more?

Her eyes still held me tight in their gaze — searching for signs of who I was behind this face.

"Hmmmm..." An elongated consideration from the peanut gallery. My bleary eyes found the alchemist off to the side as they swam — pompous face pissing me off.

"You could have helped, you know," Molly glared at said pomposity. "What are you even doing here?"

"Judging," Fulcanelli did. The blowhard's entire manner was contemptuous — had been ever since we'd met at the ball.

"Judging what?" Molly snapped, her gaze alone trying to light the alchemist aflame.

"Whether I was worth St Germain's sacrifice," I gently took her hand. I wasn't sure myself. There were other ways.

I'd been the fool, but he'd paid the price for my self-imposed ignorance. If only...

Stop it. No time for those over-trodden paths. I'd fix it. Later.

"So far," Fulcanelli turned up his nose, looking down at us both, "I think not." He turned to address the path ahead. Darkened, save for a single torchlight deeper in now flickering to life.

"Ominous. That's not another trap at all." Sarcasm, I'm sure you can tell.

"Why don't you run along and trip that one as well." Asshole.

"I wouldn't deprive you of the privilege." I could be one, too.

"Boys," Molly glowered, "it's coming closer."

"So it is," Fulcanelli said through tight lips.

I stood, running through the possibilities of what the light may be. That it was coming closer meant it likely wasn't a trap so much as maybe a guard? Some other explorer — maybe lost, maybe hungry. I felt Molly's hand on mine, gripping it as I relaxed the unconscious flex — releasing a sword I no longer held.

"Would you like to buy a book?" The voice in the dark, oddly mellow and slightly hypnotic — sad, yet simultaneously hopeful. I heard the rhythmic scrape of leather on stone shortly after the overt solicitation and felt the need to give the peddler wide berth.

"Not today, I think," I said after a brief consideration. "Perhaps another."

"But..." Molly started with the puppy dog eyes, "...books." Delight.

The last alchemist remained silent, yet stood rigidly beside us — gone was the languid casualness with which he'd approached our trip thus far. I redoubled my suspicions — for good measure.

"Oh," the peddler deflated a bit, coming closer into view. His pack was laden high as he stooped forward, nearly toppling under the weight. The lantern lighting his way dangled from the ponderous top, swaying with each step — casting his face in dancing shadows.

Oblivious to our misgivings, he carefully lowered his pack stacked high with tomes — taller than he — and took out a tiny folding stool to sit, positioning himself to display his wares.

"They're fresh from the Scriptorum," he smiled, wizened face crinkling. "Just picked them up. Perfect for any librocubicularist." He flipped the pages of the freshly antique bound books, wafting the scent of tattooed trees toward Molly — now creeping closer to the sun-browned man and his tantalizing wares. I supposed he didn't always live in a cave. Er, lair, labyrinth, whatever you wanted to call it.

I intercepted, engaging the unnerving peddler. Who set up shop in a trap-filled labyrinth?

"Any unwritten?" I forced composure as I perused the makeshift shelf slung from his back — a freshly unwritten tome might be just the trick.

"An unwritten book?" Molly perplexed at the idea. "How does that even happen?" Ever wondered why normies collect journals? Instinct.

"Blind monks writing backward." I ran my finger along the leather spines — saying it as if it were the simplest thing, despite the knowledge not being there prior to my saying it.

Hints and trickles of it had been enough for Elliot to engage my services. The dragon-cat had apparently trusted me within his horde of books because of those drabbles that had surfaced over the years, picking up the subconscious hints I'd been putting down.

To say Elliot had been frustrated when he sought my help would be an understatement. The Age of Enlightenment had been wondrous for the bibliophile — the exponential proliferation of knowledge a heady dream as books no longer became a rarity. But as with all such progress, new problems developed, and worms were not the only creatures feasting on the treasured pages.

Though, imps didn't exactly eat the pages themselves, rather the writing on them — devouring the tasty, tasty words. And what they left behind was just wrong. Inane drivel even the most Shakespearean monkey wouldn't fling against the page. Though rumor has it his folios got infested before being properly protected — commoner that he was — and did a number on *Two Gents* and parts of others.

It's funny, people ridicule the marginalia, but really they had a purpose — wards. Protection against the imps. All the snails and weird rabbit knights served to fight off the infection, or at least draw them away from the text as a whole. That's why you sometimes get naked duck sailors and trumpet farters and the totally weird-ass cats — an imp infestation nipped in the bud. Trapped in the absurdity of the images. These days, people just draw that fancy diamond 'S' on page corners.

And when they eventually went away after Johnny made his press, so did their protections, leading to Elliot's current predicament.

"No, no," the peddler distasted. Damn. Save us a trip if he did. "Improper, those," he continued in his papery voice, haughty now. His face wrinkled even further in a pucker, trying to turn itself inside out. "Unpleasant," he shuddered.

"This isn't right." Molly had sneakily snuck around my blockade and now thumbed through some volumes on the stack. I don't know if it was because she was Trenynn and had an affinity for the pages, reading through osmosis, or if she was just that voracious a reader, but she straight up *absorbed* the words on the page.

Molly's eyes flickered to mine as her jaw snapped shut, cutting whatever blatant observation she was about to make short. Thank goodness, she was learning.

"Let me see." I took the tome from her hands, rifling through the pages of the scribed words of Mary Shelly. In it... well, it was just wrong. I could feel writhing in the pages. They smelled of almonds — as did he. "Fresh from the Scriptorium, you say?" I quirked an eyebrow. For being bound in the antique style, there were no marginalia. Barely any drop caps at that.

"Oh, yes, yes," the thin, papery voice crinkled. "Would you like to buy this fine rendition?" Hopeful eyes met mine. Desperate. Hungry.

I kept them on me, motioning Molly to move away. It'd finally clicked into place — why my hackles had raised and Fulcanelli disengaged. You see, when an imp is left to glut, it grows bold — bloated beyond the boards binding the pages. And this one was trying to spread. I didn't particularly want to see what happened if a burgeoning imp spread its tendrils to a bookish Trenynn.

On one level, I felt for the peddler. No doubt he once was a hopeful writer, spirit now corrupted — consumed. The reasons were always different — anger, depression, regret, envy, spite. I'm particularly fond of spite, myself, but my words are on the page — more than most can say — even if they're oft overlooked.

Not everyone is so fortunate. And I felt like a total dick pulling the line everyone hates hearing, but needs must.

"Maybe later." I smiled and started waving around the labyrinthine lair hallway. "We just got here," I expanded my gesture to include Molly and, reluctantly, Fulcanelli, "so we're just doing our lap." I smiled broader through the put-off and motioned Molly to go on behind my back. "Want to see what all's around, you know?"

The peddler's wrinkled face folded further in confusion. He opened his mouth for a comeback.

I kept laying it on, though. "Really cool stuff!" I emptied my eyes — nearly going Hylic — and gave him a glazed look of disinterest that fractured his resolve. "Very talented," mimicking every placating lookie-loo I'd ever met across the table — the ones who never intended to even *consider* buying anything. "I'll definitely think about it," I wouldn't, walking backward before he was able to shoot down any of my objections. He was crumbling.

Quickly we ducked into the darkness, mindful of any following flickers of light.

The only thing that did was a muted "oh" as the peddler's impish heart broke just a little bit.

"What kind of nonsense was that?" Further along now — nothing more transpiring — Molly apparently piped up.

"Rather curious myself." Fulcanelli spared me a quizzical eye as we walked. Head on discreet swivel, the alchemist kept the other out for traps. Not that any found would necessarily be shared.

"Need to take you to a con sometime," I laughed — you heard it all too often. And it was soul-crushing every single time.

"We've run dozens of cons," Molly began. "I figure we're..."

"Different kind of con," I jumped ahead of the side track I'd not meant to form.

"*How??* That shouldn't have worked," Fulcanelli steered us back.

"But it did," I countered factually. "As for how... don't know," I lied with a shrug — emotional damage for-the-win. "Had a hunch."

"A *hunch*," Fulcanelli scandalized, looking now to Molly for shared outrage.

"What's the big deal?" Molly, dear Molly, took this in stride like most other things I do — especially when they do work. Why worry when it works? Wasted effort that.

"Do you *know* what that thing," Fulcanelli spat for emphasis, "was likely to do?"

"No," Molly didn't rise to the bait. "Did it *do* it?"

"It could have..." the alchemist began, stopping short to answer the actual question asked, not the one presumed. Ass. "No. It didn't, but it..."

"If it didn't, then it doesn't matter," Molly cut off the forthcoming lecture. Seemed Fulcanelli was on her shit list now, poor bastard. "What's next?" She brightened as she turned to me.

"I'd have said we storm the library and conscript a book unwritten," I grinned, somewhat roguishly. Molly giggled at the hyperbole — at least, I hoped she thought I was hyperbolic. "But that mess has me worried what we'll find."

"What's so special about it being *unwritten*?"

"Imp trap." I said it matter-of-factly, leading us further down the hall into the unknown. We should have been seeing lights from iron wall sconces by now, but they stood empty... "OW! Son of a..." and invisible in the darkness.

Fulcanelli snickered, somehow navigating the total dark with utter grace. For that matter, Molly hadn't misstepped, either, that I could tell.

I should probably know that trick. I think. Not remembering how to do stuff sucks. But then... remembering other things sucks worse.

Like what I'd done to Gregory and his brood. I shivered, suppressing the memory before I felt the viscous yolk spatter across...

Molly found my hand in the dark, bringing me back. "Ahem. Should go without saying leave no trace means not denting the fixtures in addition to packing out your trash," she smarmed. I don't know if she'd sensed me drifting places I oughtn't, or just felt like patronizing me — probably both. "And we're walking," she pulled me forward into the unseen.

"On your left, you'll not see a beautifully intricate stone wall," she carried on with the tour guide. "It dates from the Marinoan glaciation — the stone, not the wall — when it was ripped out of some unnamed mountain range and..."

"Would you kindly curtail the prattle?" Fulcanelli bristled in the oppressive dark. The heat from the alchemist's perturbed gaze would have lit the entire hallway, had it any tinder ready to catch. As it was, it threatened to singe the hairs on my neck.

"If you'd *kindly* contribute something besides brooding silence, certainly." Withering rebuttal. Check.

"I'm not certain I *should*, given the circumstances."

"And what circumstances are those," she prod on. "Who was that, and why'd you all the sudden get a stick up your ass? You sit on that broom?" Rare form. I could imagine the hand on her hip and defiant cock of her head as she lashed out with her tongue. Certainly no shrinking violet — in the traditional sense. The actual botany, though...

"Ones that are not good," Fulcanelli ground between his teeth. "I'd go so far as to say they were, in fact, fairly bad."

"He's not wrong," I reluctantly added, feeling Molly's hand tighten. It wasn't often I admitted things were bad — there was always a way.

The entire traipse down the hallway, I'd been running through possibilities in my head, racking my brain for a solution for scenarios that weren't — all while Molly filled the void. None were good, but nothing I'd conjured required a silent approach, either, so I felt it best to maintain the lively spirit as long as we could. Molly was a marvel in that regard.

Dena had always been good at that, too. Whenever I'd lost myself in shadow, she'd been the light showing me the way.

"You really know how to..." Molly began.

"Shush!" Fulcanelli interrupted.

"Now just a minute," Molly worked up.

"Wait," I said a bit more gently. "Listen."

We fell silent. None moved, nor dared to breathe. I'd heard something, too. A scrabbling sound deeper in the pitch black.

I really hoped it wasn't a grue.

Thankfully, no grue waited deeper in the cavern darkness, only in my head. The maze end held instead a creaking doorway, darker still inside. I risked a light, striking alchemist fire to life. Purple on black — normally flattering — lent an ominous air to an already foreboding scene while doing absolutely nothing to actually illuminate the situation through the Scriptorum doorway.

That, at least, *was* illuminated — the plaque by the door frame declaring the Scriptorum had been established pre-Papacy. When, exactly, wasn't clear, but it'd been protecting the written word for a millennium or two — depending on which Pope the bronze plate referred to — and now it was laid bare to the cold stones.

Again, something scrabbled in the murk — a shadow now, flicking past the opening in a brief flutter. Chains rattled and clattered, following the flitting shadow across.

Great. They were loose.

Among other literary services, the Scriptorum took in imp-infested books — like Elliot's — and restored them. Set the words right again. But sometimes, a tome was too far gone, and those became part of the Bound collection.

Have you ever seen the chained library at Hereford? Back when books were rare and much more valuable — monetarily speaking — they were kept under lock and key, chained to the shelves since security tags hadn't quite been invented yet.

These particular books were chained for other reasons, though. Deemed too dangerous, corrupting, or too far gone from an infestation, they were sequestered away in quarantine — which now seemed to be broken as another chained shadow fluttered heavily across the door, seeking a freedom still denied.

"Where are the damnedable scribes?" Fulcanelli grimaced, fully aware of the fuckery going about. While the scribes *were* blind, they at least kept some courtesy lights on for visitors. Typically.

"Smoke break?" Molly laughed through the tension, nervous energy flowed through her grip.

"Filthy habit," I joked, stepping forward into the violet dark.

Around me more chains rattled, nervous as well. The scuttling, scrabbling sounds ceased, wary of intrusion, perhaps. No shadowy lumps showed on the floor, so maybe the scribes weren't dead — at least not dead here. Fled then? Fled what?

"How's ya boi!"

I jumped at the squawk from the shelf behind me. I held the indigo flame higher, seeing a bird I was rather familiar with in an unfamiliar setting.

"How's ya boi," it repeated from atop a stack, not a bowler hat. Wings fluttered as the round man's parrot landed on my shoulder.

"That's a very good question I should like the answer to," I told the parrot.

A warm glow lit the room, bathing the bird in full technicolor. "Found the guest lights," Fulcanelli congratulated himself. "Oh, that's not good," the alchemist said upon seeing the bird.

"Nope," I agreed for once. "Very not good."

"Why's it not good?" Molly puzzled, reaching to pet the bird. All the things.

"Because he's not sitting on a short round fel…" Idea. "Molly, ask him where his boss is."

She locked eyes with the parrot on my shoulder. My gaze traveled between the two, imagining little woo-woo lines as they psychically conversed — or however that worked for Molly.

"Nothing," Molly blinked. "All I get is an image of cards shuffling in pudgy hands."

Fulcanelli grimaced, opening previously pursed lips to speak. I held up a hand to stay the coming complaint.

"Anything written on the cards?"

She shook her head. "Just blank."

"How's ya boi?" The parrot preened nervously, plucking an errant feather. "DeWitt," he changed it up.

Fulcanelli glared my way, still holding a thought in the pattern. I waved it clear for landing.

"The Index is missing," the alchemist stated the not-so-obvious. "You know what that means..."

I didn't. Not really. I should, probably. Alarm bells were certainly ringing in my head, and I was concerned for someone I called friend, but as for the greater meaning of the little man's absence, I'd still forgotten. But I probably shouldn't let that show, so I kept my face blank, slightly perturbed yet non-committal.

Keeping my damn mouth shut — a trick that'd well served me many lifetimes — I walked deeper among the shelves, ignoring the eyes piercing my backside, focusing instead on the parrot's claws punching into my shoulder. Guess that's why the short chap wore a bowler hat — probably armored.

The books were unsettled, rattling chains as I passed. Each working up the gumption to make a break for it despite the watching eyes now present. Pages riffled and spines flexed in their bindings, testing iron.

A thought unsettled me, too late, as the Scriptorum door slammed shut.

The Tipping Scales

YOU SEE, IMPS WEREN'T the only things locked away in the Scriptorum — there were darker things held in the pages.

Unsettling things.

"I suppose it's too late to say we should go," Fulcanelli with the obvious.

"How 'bout being a little more helpful?" Molly seethed in the alchemist's face. "Can you maybe do that? Great. Thanks," she dragged out, turning before the little volcano could erupt.

"Maybe when you start being useful," Fulcanelli muttered — ignored by Molly, thank goodness. Really didn't need that blow up. Not when...

Well, I wasn't sure exactly what was loose among the shelves of the Scriptorum, but it was enough to scare the books — to make them suddenly desire to flee after years of complacent confinement. So, not good. Of the things held here, perhaps a vore of some sort...

"I am here to drink the color from the leaves, please."

Damn, wrong again.

The fluttering of butterfly wings accompanied the sudden voice as a warm breeze flowed through the chamber deep underground. Loose pages I hadn't noticed on the floor rustled. Molly froze. Chains rattled loudly against shelves — the books were quivering. So was she.

"How's ya boi!" Bad timing. At least it didn't reply with 'DeWitt' — really didn't want the bird giving the ginger fairy permission.

Sparks of warm light seeking our souls flowed toward the bird, coming to gleam in one of its beady eyes, dark as the abyss. Far too close to my face for comfort.

Chill followed close after the warm breeze, and with it, not a small fae creature as we'd seen in the forest clearing nigh on to Samhain. Rather, long legs swept a tall creature toward us. Orange motes of autumn sunlight kicked up in her wake. Wings of a monarch draped sensuously down her back. She radiated hunger as one hand trailed along the shelf of Bound books, seemingly selecting her next victim.

I motioned for everyone to keep their damn mouths shut and not move a muscle. Probably unnecessary, seeing as Molly was still pinned in place, but you can't be too careful.

Fae lights twinkled and twirled, settling on the chain of one book in particular, swarming the iron links until they rusted through — crumbling to free the tome at the touch of the ginger fairy's nimble fingers.

Less ephemeral and far more *present* than she'd been in the fell forest I'd met her last, the ginger fairy grinned wide at her selection — all teeth and tongue — pulling the leather-bound book from the shelf on which it'd been imprisoned. I couldn't make out the gilt lettering in the dim light, but I could see the gleam of hunger in her eyes. Her tongue languidly licked the air, flexing to the tip of her nose in gross anticipation of the tome she was about to consume.

Disconcerting me most, though, was that she did all this with Molly's face. Gone were the pinched features of the minor fae, grown full with avaricious... lust? What *else* had she been eating? A nymph or two? Succubus maybe? The bit of Molly's soul she'd supped away couldn't account for this rapacious growth. Nor could even the stoutest stand of woodland.

Besides, it wasn't even the right season. The fuck was going on?

Distracted, pondering the possible causes, I'd not noticed Molly boiling over until I heard a clipped 'That *bitch!*' breeze by my ear.

She'd not been frozen by fear, no. Rather, rage, barely contained.

No longer.

Molly grabbed one of the bound volumes by the chain, ripping it off the shelf with implacable strength — the restraining bolts tearing free of the wood. The book itself she unkindly freed from its chain, winging it at the ginger fairy's head while she wrapped the links around her fist.

The iron side of the bound book struck the fae creature, drawing sparks of orange and causing it to recoil at the ferrous sting.

Molly pressed her advantage, jumping at the stunned soul sucker — tackling it to the ground and beating its face.

The fairy blinked — shrinking for a moment to its original size, slipping the pin — and pumped its monarch wings away from the onslaught. Molly had none of it. She bent unnaturally and grabbed the creature by its copper hair, flinging it into a shelf. The sizzle as the iron spines burned the now tiny fae made me cringe.

The wee creature whimpered, fluttering to the ground. Gone were the glittering orange sparks of her passing, muted as she coughed.

Molly stalked toward the fallen fairy, grabbing it by the monarch wings. I ducked a ladder, going after her before she went too far.

"Why?" she demanded, shaking the small body. "Why drink from me? The Pact still holds sway…" Molly stared into the shrunken version of her own face, searching for some answer. Some meaning to her trauma.

"Hungry," a small whisper came. "Dead, all gone. Need the color from the leaves, please." Delirium had taken hold.

I reached out, grasping Molly's tense hand. I knew that look. She wanted to do *things* to this being — very un-Molly-like things.

"They have a history, I take it," Fulcanelli opened his damn mouth to droll.

"Bit. But that's in the past," I assured Molly. "She can't hurt you." The un-Molly-ness lingered.

It's not like she was a pacifist or anything — she gave back twice what she got — but this creature was defenseless. The ginger fairies, in general, were a nuisance more than real threat — unless you were an evergreen. Its behavior before had been passing strange as it was — before I even knew Molly was Trenynn — given that they hardly ever interacted with people. And now it was awake well before time. I reiterate: the fuck?

"Molly." I held her hand still, gingerly reaching for the fairy in her grasp.

Truth be told, I wanted to squish it myself, the little vermin, but it had no idea exactly what trouble it caused with an errant kiss. I was trying to be better myself, and I didn't want Molly to have that regret.

"OW Fuck!" I clenched the fairy in my fist hard as it bit my thumb — needle teeth digging in to draw blood. Shit. I let go of the squished fae and flung it to the floor, freeing my hand.

"That bitch!" Like it was her name. Molly stalked forward again, cycle on the verge of repeat until Fulcanelli intervened, stepping on the fairy, fully intending to squish it. Ruthless bastard.

And missed.

Double fuck. My blood.

This would be out of hand way too soon if I didn't do *something* — stupid or drastic, I hadn't decided which yet in that particular nanosecond. And yep... the damn thing was growing again.

Only one thing to do — cheat. And quick.

The fairy, grown once more to human size, slipped on a discarded book leaf and stumbled into a shelf, perfectly tangling its arms in the binding chains. I stepped in, wrapping more chains around its waist, legs, and — most importantly — sharp-toothed mouth before it could work itself free, snapping the hasp of a lock closed to seal the deal.

"You did that a little too quickly, Felix." Molly eyed her ginger twin chained to the shelves.

"Just thought you two had practiced..." Fulcanelli started to quip before shutting the hell up at both of our looks. It wasn't like that, not with Molly. Maya... maybe a time or two... but that's not the story at hand.

"Had to," I sucked my thumb. It'd been a while since I bled. "She'd have slipped either of you." They both glanced at my hand. Fulcanelli frowned, knowing. Molly scrunched up her face, guessing.

"So it would seem," the alchemist broke the silence, weighing the implications of the situation. "Well then," changing gears, "you best both be gone."

Distant, I heard bells ringing and boots crunching.

Not again.

"Don't they have anything else better to do than bother me?" Whoever *they* were this time — I lose track. SSDT — same shit, different they.

"Not really, no," the alchemist drolled, eying me. "But I do doubt this response is for you — directly, at least," shifting gaze toward the bound fairy, struggling against the irons. In its larger form, the touch seemed to burn less — more surface area, I guess? — but it definitely seemed quite irate, glaring over the biting chain.

"Fan-fucking-tastic," I grumbled. We hadn't even found what we'd come for yet. Which actually wasn't what we came for, but since the monks were gone — or dead — we couldn't exactly get Elliot's books we'd tucked away in the twist fixed. Have to settle for imp-poison instead.

"Molly, go look on the stands for a book with blank pages. I'll check the shelves. Fulcanelli, grab the ginger," I started — knowing Molly shouldn't, and I couldn't risk it getting another piece of me — tangent, how the fuck? — so that left the alchemist.

"No." Plain and simple. No.

"You said it yourself," I puzzled, "we have to go."

"You," the alchemist said. "Not we. I will be staying right here to keep an eye on *that*, while you beat a hasty retreat.

"Furthermore," Fulcanelli turned to Molly before I got an edgewise word, "I'd suggest you stay here, or anywhere far away from him, really. You seem nice and it'd be terrible to get you caught up in his..." the alchemist gestured vaguely at my general personage "...persona non-grata status."

I mean. It was fairly sound advice — advice I'd been trying to impart on her since the beginning — but it irked me hearing it come from someone else's mouth.

"What's everyone got against Felix?" I guess it was time she asked. Past time.

"Haven't you noticed that bad luck besets any close to him and follows wherever his shadow touches?" Fulcanelli returned to the Scriptorum door, checking outside for responding guards. Bells still rang, now less distant — though not by much. It should take a minute more — familiar as they were with the tunnels and traps, they still had to make their way through the labyrinth same as we had.

"No," Molly perplexed, rummaging around recent memory. "In fact, Felix has always been pretty lucky for me," she smiled my way. "Pulled my butt out of the fire more than once."

"Oh, the irony of that name," the alchemist dramatized. "*Felix Chance*," putting some stank on it, "Mister Lucky Good Luck he named himself. Tell me, who put your rear to the flame to begin with?"

"None of that was his fault." Molly set her hip, stopping her search for the unwritten.

"Oh, but it was," Fulcanelli countered. "That's how it works — the world always in balance, and he," jabbed a finger at me, "tips the scales."

My friend, cohort, and oft co-conspirator bit her lip, thinking through the order of our events. "Felix?"

"He's not wrong," I admitted, busying myself in the stacks. We didn't have time for this. "But it's not that simple either." Where were the unwritten?

"It is, *dear boy*." More stank. "Case. In. Point," -ing around the current mess. "The Scriptorum. A sanctum, centuries inviolate, and soon as you come poking your nose," Fulcanelli barely kept a lid on it, worked up nearly to froth.

"How's ya boi," the parrot interrupted for good measure. I heard boots echoing louder.

"And now the Index is missing as well." Nearly at a loss, but not quite. "Of course. Trouble loves you."

"What's the Index?" Molly looked up from browsing the books.

"Who," I supplied. "The Index of the Akashic Record. Keeper of all knowledge — and some say the universe itself." Real-life Tommy Westphall, the little round man.

"Sounds kinda important," Molly with the understatement of the millennium. "I'm not seeing any blank books," she frowned, back on topic. "These all have pictures." She held up a blue leather-bound book, flipping through the illuminated pages.

"That's perfect!" I checked the tome myself. "No words, lots of marginalia to trap the imps," I appraised. "This will do nicely."

"Would you like to buy a book today?" The thin, papery voice scratched its way down the dark hallway, halting the crunch of boots in their tracks. Bless the imp who bought us a few more seconds with his pestering.

I slammed the door shut again before I could hear what happened next — things probably did not go too well for the escaped imp.

"Is there another way out?" I leaned my back against the door, fixing it in place a bit longer as I looked around the trashed sanctuary. Finally, my eyes landed on Fulcanelli, standing silent — weighing options.

On the one hand, sharing a way out would be helping me, which the alchemist seemed vehemently against — at least until my worthiness had been judged. But on the other, aiding in my escape would get me well out of that ginger hair on Fulcanelli's head — which was no doubt highly appealing.

"How'd that *bitch*," still with all the stank, "get in?"

"Good question," I considered. One of the fair folk never would have made it through the front — even if it'd somehow slipped a ride in a monk's robe, and this little one didn't seem that clever. Also, had the creature done something to the monks? Highly unlikely — it seemed more opportunist than malicious. Desperate as well, driven and afraid come stumbling into succor.

Many good questions — all springing to mind at once.

"Let's find out, shall we?" Fulcanelli focused, plucking a hair from the ginger fairy's head and rummaged overly long in a too-deep pocket before withdrawing a polished spiral shell, glowing nearly iridescent in the Scriptorum's dim light.

I let out a low whistle — where the hell had the rat bastard come across *that*?

"Where did you come from, little austice?" Better than bitch, I'd guess, but that was the totally wrong thing to say to the gingery fairy. It freaked the fuck out, struggling against the iron searing delicate skin, eyes going wild as it screamed around the chain between its teeth.

MMPH. "No go back." PHHRM. "Bad. No." EEEGH.

"Maybe it was a bear drill," I said before the panic spread. Though in retrospect, that might not have been the most calming notion if you didn't know the, well, drill — all bookshops in London have them. Worked to break the tension, though — all eyes shot to me. "Anyone find the hi-viz tabards?" I kept on the non-sequitur, adding, "And if it is an actual bear emergency, Molly can talk to it," I charmed. "Ask it not to eat us."

"How's ya boi?"

"Off his rocker, apparently," Molly reflexively replied. At least she wasn't panicking.

"Concur," Fulcanelli agreed, still preparing the thaumaturgic shell — working the fairy's hair into a harness for the ant — don't ask me where it'd come from, I was distracted by my own distracting — at the opening.

Even the fairy calmed a bit, realizing we weren't sending it whence it came. That apparent stupidity was reserved for me — Molly would insist her, too, despite suggestions to the contrary. Just try and stop her.

Cooler head holding sway once more, she turned her attention back to the alchemist at work. Now sealing the shell opening with a wax stopper and smearing something sweet-smelling on a tiny hole on the opposite end of the nautilus.

"As above, so below, huh?" Fundamental principle of alchemy. Not sure if that was rule number one, or if that honor belonged to *If I lick it, it's mine.*

"As within," Fulcanelli held up the shell, sprinkling a fine powder across the tiny opening. "So without." Glimmering red sparks coalesced into a sinuous beam of light, snaking off into the Scriptorum stacks — strangely enough. I'd expected the bear escape route to be deeper in the darkness.

"Daedalus thread," I side-mouthed for Molly's sake. She'd seen a lot palling around with St Germain, but I doubted this ancient trick was part of his alchemical crash course. "Handy, that."

Fulcanelli waited a moment for the strand of fate to pull taut, hooking destiny like a trout by the mouth. "Ah, there we go." No further word, the alchemist led among the rows of books, chains rattling as we passed. They were still afraid, but not quite like before — settling now that the fairy was caught. And whatever bear that let the creature in, gone.

One book lay askew on the shelf, spine broken neatly in two as the fore-edges remained bound.

"Rivers of Avon," Molly read, picking up the flayed book — the crimson thread dove straight into its pages.

"Not redundant at all," I smarmed. Like ATM Machine.

"Romans." Eyes rolled. Mine. Molly's. The parrot's.

"Pick a card," the parrot changed it up. The bird squawked from the shelf before briefly taking flight to dig razors into my shoulder — no wonder he wore a hat. "DeeeeWitt," returning to a familiar phrase, wings flapping again.

"What card?" I asked as I felt an unexpected bulge in my pants — one I wasn't happy about. It felt peculiarly like a stack of three-by-fives. "Oh," I reached into my pocket. "Horn if you're honky," I read from the neatly typed index card strangely in my pocket. "Super helpful," I side-eyed the bird.

"Where..." Fulcanelli started, eyes wide.

SHPOP! The vault door's seal broke with a whoosh and the groan of heavy hinges.

"I guess they come with the bird." Thankful for the distraction drawing the alchemist's attention. I didn't want to think about the import or gravity or significance of any of it right then. "We need to be gone." I tucked the nonsensical card back into my pocket. "Like, now."

"Great, how? It's a dead end." Molly held up the splayed halves of the leather-bound Rivers into which the sparkling red thread fled.

"Not quite." Something slithering on the pages caught my eye. "Here." I tugged at the corner of a loosened page, teasing a full signature from the codex threads.

"Put your backs into it," a gruff voice muffled over the shuffling of feet, echoing through the stacks as the stuck door complained at their mistreatment. *Just a bit longer.*

The pages folded over by fourths unfurled, flowing the disparate rivers together into one formed anew of dancing ink limned with red as the thread coiled into the page like a whirlpool. The map grew larger as it sucked the thread in, falling to the floor with the flop of thick parchment being unrolled.

"Well, in you go." Fulcanelli kindly kicked me from behind as I stupidly bent to study the spreading *terra incognita*. Have I mentioned he's a thrice-damned asshole?

I had a long time to fall as the world spun over me — at least, it felt like a long time. I don't think the full nine-point-eight applies when falling into maps laid upon the floor — not after you cross planes.

Maybe it was the adrenaline suddenly pumping through my blood at, well, falling through a reality or two. Lots happened on the other side of that hole in the sky.

Too much.

Molly lunged. Fulcanelli grabbed. Dislodged, the parrot clawed.

I got mad. Really mad. Do-something-stupid mad.

"*Puttana ingrata,*" Fulcanelli spat at Molly, who now bristled with thorns — slipping his bleeding grip. She leapt through the hole in the fractured sky.

Good girl.

I reached past her, cheating by blood-proxy — exploding the tableau into chaos with the ginger fairy entering the fray. Bastard deserved it.

Last I saw before the hole closed, the alchemist fell from sight — the ginger fairy planting a kiss.

Lost in the Spoom

"WHY'D YOU DRAW THE curtains?" Molly looked disappointed — and slightly green. Not because she was sick or anything, but...

It was our fourth night in the wylde and our first finding any sort of shelter, much less a full-on cabin. Don't worry — I'd knocked and none answered. Thrice.

"A measure of protection," I muttered. The darkness outside didn't like to be seen.

Molly laughed, caressing the finely carved wood of the cabin walls. The figures put me in mind of Orym and Dain — or their kin. Mental note to observe *all* the guest rites — there are rules to these things. Aid and succor is never withheld in these parts, if it can be found, but you have to be polite about it and never take more than you offer.

"I don't think we really need protection, Felix." Molly's eyes flashed green. "Not here." The last few nights had unnerved her a bit, causing the subtle reversion to her Trenynn self off-season — an unconscious flex in self-defense.

"True," I offered, still pulling the curtains — shutting away the not-so-empty dark.

It needed the break.

Molly's presence was one thing — she belonged among the wood in the wylde. Welcomed and warmly familiar. She'd have been perfectly fine, power move or no — had she been alone.

Me?

Well, I'd be fine, too, but I wasn't welcome or wanted — too foreign, too other to their nature. Set the bumpers' teeth on edge, did I, and being out in the open the last three nights had worn their nerves thin.

I shuttered the last portal onto the forest green and felt a palpable sigh of relief from the night outside — my presence finally concealed.

Like I said, only polite.

One thing I'd learned of late — those ominous, foreboding feelings I'd picked up on wherever I went? I hadn't known what they meant after the waters of Lethe wiped the pains away, but I'd been given a smidgen of insight of late. Defense mechanisms. The bumpers were scared.

Of me.

Turns out they were mostly harmless — all scary teeth and gnashy shadows set to chill. Sure, they could do some damage — and some, like Bill, delighted in it — gutting the unwary traveler too stupid to breathe and who ran afoul of kitting wylde ones. But those were isolated incidents — usually, they just wanted to be left the hell alone. And while one idiot come upon in a dark wood was easy prey, historically, torch-bearing and pitchfork-wielding mobs proved quite lethal.

Or at least annoying.

So they kept concealed, rustling the bushes and preying more upon the imagination than actual faces.

"Pretty lucky," Molly twirled in the space — a bit giddy from the flush green surrounding our little haven, "finding this cabin like that." Her eyes unsettled on me — emeralds set with rubies — as sprigs of sharp leaves framed her face.

"Nice place," I deflected. And it wasn't — not directly. "Little disused, but cozy."

Dust, like snow, layered deep — softening everything in a blanket of grey. Obscuring the simple artifacts on the mantle — the key to a lock, swirls and curls of drawn silver; an ivory comb, finely engraved and yellowed with age; and a penny, stamped by one of those amusement park machines.

"You know it's a trap, right?" Molly sprawled herself out on the leather couch — a gentle dust cloud rose in protest.

"There's whisky!" The key had not opened the liquor cabinet — that stood open. Good stuff, too.

"Aren't you listening?" Molly threw a throw at me, pillow nearly knocking the bottle out of my hand. "Don't touch the booze! You wanna get stuck here?"

"I know the rules," I said around the cork in my teeth. *Helped write them,* I didn't add. "And the owner." I poured a finger for the both of us, taking Molly a glass. "I think."

"You think?" Eying the glass with great suspicion, she still took it.

I eyed the intertwined horseshoes over the door, pointing with my glass.

"Is that iron?" One was, certainly.

"And silver," I said of the other.

"The silver I get, but what's with the iron?" Molly moved to check the charms. "They can't touch the stuff," she sipped the whisky.

"Cast in the fires of dawn and dusk.

Forged in shadow of the slivered moon's bow.

A binding spell, a silent ward,

Worked with love, the metals flow."

"Nemli's curse," I recited. "This is good," I side-tracked back to the whisky. A nice scotch, probably a highland. "Fruity and mellow."

"Nemli?" Molly didn't take the bait, though she did sip the scotch — her nose crinkled in delight.

"Long story," I didn't go into it. Lots of trauma there — and for once, not my own! "And we need to figure out what to do about this situation. Still got the cards?"

High time we did something stupid.

Well, stupid-er... I guess. Not that that's really a word, but I'll make it one for now.

We'd gotten lost in the spoom — thanks to being kicked into the map upside down. Grumble — when we made our escape from the Scriptorum. Every which way we'd turned had been wrong and the wylde had simply delighted in turning us around.

I swear, the only reason we found the cabin was because that dumb catgirl tried to point us the wrong direction, which actually was the right direction. Bless her heart and that single brain cell shared among all orange cats.

What do you call a group of catgirls? Herd? I know you can herd cats, not that I'd really want to. Anyway, whatever they're called, we stumbled on a group of them yowling the second evening.

"Girl, I had four of them by the time I was twenty one," a fiery black-haired catgirl proudly proclaimed.

"Fertile-Myrtle here," another purred, calico coat dripping from her shoulders. "How many grands now?" She sipped an umbrella drink.

"Three litters," she grinned wicked sharp teeth. "It's a ratchet picture, but here's the lot of 'em." She passed around a cracked phone to many *awwws* and other declarations of cuteness.

A fair-furred cat swiped the screen. "Quite a mixed brood," she smarmed.

"You know how it goes," Myrtle — we'll call her — snatched the phone back with a smoky side-eye before the other swiped further. "Wanna switch husbands for a bit?"

"Stooooop," they yowled in unison, falling over in drunken laughter. Not getting involved.

"Hi there!" The aforementioned orange flipped down from the branch above us before Molly and I could make our retreat.

She landed in a crouch between us, coming up with a catty smile — her tufted ears twitched as her blue eyes locked onto me. Molly prickled, her crown of leaves growing sharp points.

"Where've you been, Elillie?" Cover blown, one of the yowlers came to the spot where we'd stopped. "Who're you?" Drunk, the vertical slits of her eyes uneven in their accusation.

"They're my new friends!" The tabby glommed onto me, licking my cheek. "Well, he is," she threw Molly shade, "she smells funny." Elillie — I guess that was her name — veritably vibrated as she leaned in closer.

"Get your hands off..." Molly didn't finish her thought as she launched a swipe at the pawsy catgirl.

"Mrowl!" Elillie launched herself out of the way with a cattish laugh, landing lightly to wrap her arms around Molly. "Don't be jealous," she purred, "there's plenty of snuggles for yo... owwwlnyahiss!!"

They both bristled — thorny leaves sprouting from Molly's shoulders, cascading down her back; meanwhile, orange fur bristled sharp as steel spikes as Elillie fell to all fours, her back arching.

"Alright, break it up!" I brandished a squirt bottle at the both of them, squeezing the trigger a hair — sending a slight mist at the tabby.

"Seems our Elillie isn't the only one in heat." The fiery black feline cackled in delight, interposing her drunken self between the two. "Come to the fire," she looped an arm through mine. "You won't need that," she patted my hand holding the sprayer.

A strange glint filled the orange's blue eyes as we passed — small smile spreading across her face as she sat, licking her wounded paw. Kinky girl.

I brandished the bottle at her for good measure before vanishing it in the twist — she shivered as she groomed. Molly steered well clear of the frisky kitty, keeping her at bay with a bough of holly prickle.

"Silly boy," my escort purred close. "That'll just make her want you more. Her too," she shot Molly a smokey eye.

Been a while since anyone had called me a 'silly boy' — drunk or not. I got the feeling of agelessness from Myrtle. Three litters of grands, she'd said? The face I wore was definitely a *boy* to her — maybe even a few of my others as well. Not only does time do funny things in the wyldes of fae, but who knew what life she was on?

"You'll never snag a mate like that, kitten-britches," the calico chimed in, teasing the tabby as the rest yowled with laughter.

"Not for lack of trying," came from above as a blackbird stopped short of the ground with a mighty flap. "Just got her hoo-ha waxed and everything."

"RAVEN!" Elillie hissed as the feathered form lightly stepped to the ground, transforming into a young woman — her black pinions arranging themselves about her shoulders in a long mantle.

"I speak truth," quoth the Raven.

"Gossip, more like," Elillie huffed. "It was a test," she added defensively.

"A test for what?" Damn my curiosity.

"I feel like if I want to have a litter one day, I gotta be able to at least do this." The kinky kitty purred, swaying closer as she rubbed her inner thigh. "Wanna see?" She feigned grooming herself.

Spritz-spritz. The spray bottle was back as quick as it left. "Down, kitty."

Elillie scrowled at the mister — certainly not the facial she was after.

"Serves you right," spoke the Raven. "Not a subtle bone in your body." She spoke in the whisper of feathers. I suppressed a startle — not feeling her approach. "Here!" I certainly hadn't noticed her snapping a selfie as I'd spritzed her friend until she flashed the screen in front of my face. "Add me!"

"Wait, don't..." Too late. She posted the snap-tok-gram wherever the hell the photo went into the digital ether.

"You've got bars?" Molly'd been cut off since our escape. She'd checked. No signal. She'd probably been as itchy in digital withdrawal as I was now — I'd felt eyes on me snap open soon as the little 'woop' came from Raven's phone.

"Do now," Raven cawed.

"Storm blew through and brought a line in with it." The black cat crossed my path, leading me toward the clearing. I saw it then, the black cable snaking out of a fairy ring — no doubt twinned on the other side of the downed line.

"But it's not hooked to anything," Molly observed, pulling her phone out as we got closer.

"Doesn't really matter," I considered. "Thought that counts." I pinched my shoulders back, trying to shake the itch of all those eyes on me. Thought indeed.

"Take it down!" Elillie lunged as Raven took flight. Mentally, I sided with the cat, but it didn't really matter now — damage was done. "It makes me look stupid!"

"Not the only thing," Molly muttered. She wasn't a fan.

The catgirl ignored the remark as she launched after her feathered friend, leaping as the raven laughed from above. The herd — is that what we settled on? — of drunken catgirls fell over laughing at Elillie's antics as they sat around the fairy ring. A couple even tried to video it, but I doubted they were sober enough to actually hit record. One even had her selfie cam on, from what I could see — recording the wrong way.

"Omygosh stooooop," she complained, seeing the empty black eyes of the phones trained on her. I didn't think an orange cat could blush like that, fur growing even brighter. "You're worse than that creepy fire skeleton perving on me. Save the spray for that geezer."

Fire skeleton?

"That can't be good." Molly echoed my thought as she cringed — she and flames don't mix well.

"Probably isn't," I agreed. At the same time, I wondered exactly what a fire skeleton was, to her. I could conjure up several variations I'd encountered in past lives — the thought tickled me, a fun trick — but there's not actually a 'monster manual,' as such, for reference.

"*Sooo* not good. I was just showing him my new ghost claws... See how cute?" Elillie flexed her hand-paw-whatever, wicked sharp claws appearing from the tips. I didn't know exactly how that worked — I'm sure Molly'll fill me in later as she was entirely fascinated by the murder-toe-beans. Apparently, the catgirl did get a mani-pedi along with her Brazilian — little cartoon ghosties decorating the finger scalpels, which she danced around for Molly. "And he got this grody boner..."

Wow... the anatomical improbabilities of that sentence...

"Skibbidy toilet," quoth the Raven. Further incomprehensibilities.

"So sus," Elillie's ears twitched. "I totally should have listened to that paw reader," the train continued derailing, "but I thought she was just after some OnlyPaws action."

"Rizzin toe-beans," Raven whipped out her phone for a few snaps.

Elillie hissed and swiped playfully at the thirsty bird. "So, anyway, my hackles were all raised and I was like..."

"Is there a point to any of this?" I pinched the bridge of my nose.

"Fine, I'm not talking to you anymore," she huffed, pink nose turned up. "...but," she kept talking despite the dramatics, "that reader said to tell you that you can't leave until the bells ring."

Cryptic messages delivered by cat's paw.

Yay.

That night, the skeletons found us.

Well, sort of. What our orange furry friend neglected to mention was *how* they became skeletons in the first place, in addition to how they'd come to be on fire.

The path we'd chosen had indeed not been there until we'd set foot upon it, as the, ahem, paw reader had said by proxy, divulging itself only in whisper as we passed through unmolested.

No root rose to trip. No branch set to snag. No wayward limb gave in to gravity's sweet embrace over our heads. Though deeper in, I heard sudden rustles and crashes through the brush.

"They're scared," Molly whispered.

"Skeletons must be nearby."

"I'm not sure." She twisted her head, not quite *listening* so much as... questing? Was that the right word? Intuiting? I don't know. I just felt tendrils of energy spreading out into the wylde. "It's a different sort of fear. *l'Envoyé...?*"

d'Éternité, a bubble burst in my brain. Away in my room, the Magician grinned on the brass, teasing the key.

"The leaves are keeping hushed about this Envoy thing," her face puzzled. "What is that?"

"No idea," I lied. "What about the spooky, scary skeletons — which way are they?" I did my best David Pumpkins, stupid grin and all, hoping to distract.

"They're part of it," Molly smirked. "But not all." I'm glad she humors me, even during the tight spots. Warmth grew in my heart. Her beautiful eyes grew wide and round, glistening in the moonlight. She opened her mouth to speak, and for a moment, I saw double.

It wasn't just my heart growing warm as the crackling underbrush caught alight from the torrent of flame boiling around me. I flew forward, a weight slamming into my back.

Air burst from my chest, replaced only with flame. It wasn't that the air rushing back in was super-heated — there was no air, only burning. It felt like the flesh of my lungs was melting to congeal in my lower intestine after eating down through my diaphragm, liver, stomach... you know, all those gooey bits between. All the phlogiston in my body suddenly set loose to roam free.

I gotta say, burning from the inside out isn't terribly comfortable. Zero stars, do not recommend.

The thing that set me alight ran roughshod right over me, heat roiling from its midnight coal withers. Flames flowed behind the mare in a majestic mane as it reared before Molly, rending the air with its hooves before turning back to me.

Small blessings — Trenynn don't do well with flames, and it wasn't my first time burning alive.

My charcoaled bones creaked and cracked as I got off the damn ground. Honestly, it's a whole lot easier to move about when you don't have to worry about things like breathing and stupid physics. Nebulous flesh formed around my bones as I reached into the twist for a bucket.

I must've looked a terrible fright, flaming skeleton wreathed in plasmic goop standing off against a pyro-pony in the middle of the darkened wylde.

"Here horsie, horsie, horsie," I cooed, coaxing the mare with my red bucket. "I've got a treat for you." I shook the swishy bucket, enticing the demonspawn forward.

See, here's the thing about horses — as a general rule, they're dumber than the posts you hitch them to. Spiteful, certainly. Now, there are some exceptional equines out there, but this particular one was not — it was just mean. And hungry.

So when I offered it a bucket of tasty, tasty sand, the damn thing ate it... but only after bowling me over again to get at it.

"Umm," Molly, beside me now, "Felix?" I'm sure she had a bunch of questions I didn't feel like answering.

"Thracian Mare," I said instead, sucking in the loose phlogiston mucking about. I swear, it's like ducks — never in a row, always causing a ruckus. The mare in question started coughing and gagging on the sand — horses like sand, but it doesn't like them. "Nasty bitch," I spat as the damn thing's eyes went wide, flames roaring higher as it thrashed, trying in vain to expunge the ingested grit.

"Did you have to kill it?" Molly whined, formerly terrified eyes now plaintive.

"Did you *not* see it roast me alive?" I risked drawing the questions again, irked at the whinge. "It was a man-eater. Those other skeletons we got warned about? Appetizers."

"But horse..." She looked sadder and sadder as the flames died out in Thracian Mare's still corpse.

I swear, anything with fur — flammable or inflammable as it may be.

"Do I look a little thinner?" I'd put some meat back on my bones, but I felt some was missing.

"Horse." Forlorn. The cinders crumbled in on themselves, the last few tendrils of smoke wafting away.

"Molly-kins dear, you know better," I softened a bit, my phlogi-ducks more-or-less in a row. "Legends never die," I winked. "Just changes a bit each telling. Besides, there's like three more of the assholes. C'mon."

They weren't hard to find either. Running rampage over a little village — now entirely aflame.

Fire skeletons wandered aimlessly about, insides sous vided to taste in their own blood, waiting for the man-eating mares to nosh — guess the bitches like 'em fresh. The nightmares were distracted, though, by a body swinging in a gibbet. Poor criminal was being bat about like a ball in the iron cage — after it'd been roasted by the flames spewing from their nostrils.

"The hell is up around here?" I took a moment to appreciate just how immune to the weird Molly was now. I don't think her earlier trepidations were an act, rather just her response to new flavors of batshit. She was a tree, for goodness' sake... that was pretty odd in and of itself. But, she'd never gotten wifi in the forest — except for that one imposter tree she was telling me about once. Turned out to be a cell tower cosplaying as an oak. Should have been a pine — got caught when winter fell and its leaves, didn't.

Point is, she'd become inured to the weird kicked up in my wake through the world. Like my sudden phlogiston deficiency earlier — mostly recovered now. Or the white-robed figure floating on the air, stealthily approaching the mares from over the burning homes — Lenny wasn't going to be happy.

"Shit." Clever, I know. My vocabulary tends to degrade when faced with a death-spirit like Calley — I could never pronounce her name: Cailleach — they don't like me too very much.

"Who is tha—" I clamped my hand on Molly's mouth before she could draw the figure's focus. Fortunately, owl-face's attention was solely on the mares as she raised a hand to the coal black coat — the flaming mane hissed and froze at her touch, creature riming instantly with frost.

"Lenny's ex," I whispered. Molly's eyes widened, but she did not speak as we put on some distance. Good girl. "Calls her the Winter Hag."

"Bad breakup, I take it?" We'd ducked behind a tree.

"Wasn't good," I confirmed. "Ever wondered why he lives in the T-bird instead of fully manifesting?"

"Thought he lost a bet." Terrible gambler.

"Part of it," I admitted. "But that came after." Now he was all mopey and depressed that he was grounded. Lost a lot in the breakup. Molly'd never seen him in his storm-god-prime.

"He never came *after*," a chill voice froze the air around me. "Selfish prick."

Double shit.

"Hi Calley," I faked, peeking around the tree. The chill spirit was close now, enough to see symbols and runes delicately embroidered in electrum against the arctic white cloak. "Fancy meeting you here." Running into exes is always awkward — even if they aren't your own.

"How *is* that blowhard flash in the sack?" The frozen tone said she hoped he was a miserable wreck.

"Oh, just dandy," I lied — denying her satisfaction. "Having a grand time with tons of strippers and blow out in the desert. These kids today worship him — all kinds of festivals and shit." He actually hated them.

"I'm sure," the winter spirit looked down her hooked nose. Large eyes, round and silver as the full moon blinked unnervingly. "You can quit hiding, your friend, too. I heard you before you even came into the village."

"And you didn't kill me? How kind of you."

"Like it would have stuck," Calley scoffed, cloak rippling in the polar wind. "And her, I have nothing against." She approached Molly, hand held out. "Hello little Trenynn, you keep terrible company."

"So I've been told," Molly sighed, taking the bone white hand. She looked deeper into the hooded figure's face. "Do I know..." she started to say. Few even knew who the Trenynn were these days, but Calley was old. "Thousand-Winters," Molly suddenly bowed her head as recognition dawned. She *was* an evergreen, after all — of course she'd know the personification of winter. Or at least of her — she'd been gone a while.

"So I *am* remembered." Calley chuckled, throwing back the hood of her embroidered cloak. I got a sneaking feeling I knew what sent the ginger fairy running scared. And it was silently floating in front of the devastated village, reveling in the frigid air rolling frost across the forest floor.

"In story," Molly admitted her youth. "And," she paused in memory, "your touch. I've not felt it since before my awakening."

"That long, huh?" Calley winked. I shivered. At least she was in a passable mood. I still remembered the blizzard back in '88 when she and Lenny broke up. That was a doozy. "Men," she scoffed again.

"Not *that* long," Molly chuckled, blushing a bit at the inference.

"No," Calley cast an appraising eye, "I see not, but," she twisted her head, seeking the words.

"One of the rotvanir broke the truce," Molly growled. "And some other stuff." She shyly looked toward me.

"Just what *have* you been up to?" Icicles my way.

"Just living my life," I shrugged.

"One that was never yours," she shot. I glared.

"Finders keepers," returning fire. Suck it. "Speaking of, what're you gonna do with those?" I pointed behind her to the skeletons still shambling about, their bones now cold and frosted. Even the mares rose again with frost's bite now in their flame.

"Wouldn't you like to know?"

Wicked cold blew, chilling me to the bone.

Yes, I did want to know and she wasn't telling. But she had let us get the fuck out of there without further incident.

My luck had been running pretty thin, so I didn't really want to press it. Not with her.

Calley seemed fond of Molly — I mean, who wasn't? She's a lot more popular than I am — and I wasn't about to get all up in her business. I'd just be sure to give Lenny a heads-up she was out of lockup when we got back.

Don't ask. She's the one they named the damn loony bin after, after all. Surprised she wasn't at the ball. Totally her vibe, if wrong mythos.

Funny how that all works. Everything so similar, so connected... yet totally different. It's like I'm making this shit up.

Go figure.

"Is this a good idea?" Molly gingerly shuffled the first tarot deck. Well, first modern, popular deck. Plenty older, more sacred to some. But that one was special in its own right. Belief builds, and *that's* what people think of when you say 'tarot.' "Shouldn't you be doing this? Aren't they your cards?"

"Now *that* would be a monumentally stupid idea," I laughed. Feedback, much?

"Your speciality," she countered, giving the cards another riffle.

"You *want* the universe to blow up or something?" Probably wouldn't be quite that bad, but didn't relish a screech in existence. "No, best you do the draws. Besides, decks always attune better when gifted."

I'd gifted that particular one to Dena, once it'd been printed proper. She already had an intimate connection to the cards, having painted them, but the touch stacked.

"Fine. Cut?" she offered.

No need. I knocked once with my knuckle. A spark popped off and a card flew from the deck. See?

"Magician, reversed." Molly's eyes traveled up to meet mine.

Told you. It was mocking me.

"How about you draw three?" I wasn't touching it again.

"Page of Cups, also reversed." Insecurity, no shit. Spill the tea, why don't you? Upside down cups tended to do that.

"Remember the joy," Molly said, surprised she spoke. Love in the depths of her eyes. "Easier to face down the troubles."

"Next card?" Fates drawn to whisper.

"Cups again. Three of them." On the card one, overfull, flowed to two. At least it was upright. Party time? "Now that's better," she smiled.

"Lots of water there," I snarked as she flipped the third card over. Two cups and...

"The Chariot? But it's on land," Molly examined the card closer. "And lots of sand. Are those sphinxes?"

"Wasn't always sand."

"You're in denial," another's wry humor broke through. "Balance yourself, sweetie."

I stared down at the card... eyes drawn to the two sphinxes — one white, one black. Light and shadow. Working in tandem, they forged ahead, at odds...

The cabin door flung open, setting a gust of wind to the cards — flipping them all, shifting fates.

Not that I noticed as a mass tackled me to the wooden floor, screaming bloody murder.

"You should have died when you had the chance!"

Who the fuck are you? I wanted to shout, but the staff across my throat choking me out made that difficult.

Shadows closed in from the edge of my vision. The blood pumping in my veins begged violence — swift and messy.

Bright steel flashed before the world fell to darkness.

Whispers in the Trees

FELIX IS SCARING ME. Had been for a while now — since the pit at least. I mean, *really* scaring me. I was used to his oddities and cryptic tendencies — though that was definitely getting old — but this was different.

He does that, the echo in my soul whispered. I felt her, no lie, get a little worked up.

That? I watched as Felix impaled the bumper on his sword — where had he gotten a sword? — and shove it back out the door in a rush.

It was all a blur.

One minute, I'd been pulling cards for him to frown over — the next, some frog-wizard-looking-thing had him pinned with a staff across his throat with more shadowed figures flooding the tiny room through the shattered door.

"Waste of a staff blast," Felix had growled, twisting his hips and throwing the ragged wizard off. "Idiot," he spat before the beheading and subsequent slaughter.

I'd never seen Felix so violent before. Worse, it was a cold violence. Practical and calculated.

"Felix!" I screamed, trying to snap him out of it even as another creature leapt for his back. Danger be damned, he'd figure a way to talk us out of it like he always did.

That's what he did. Cheat.

Not always, echoed inside.

"Do you not hear the footsteps?" Fulcanelli's eyes had gone mad in the Scriptorum. I mean, he *was* mad — he'd just kicked Felix into a... book? — but then the crazy really shone through.

Footsteps? The fuck? Brief thoughts as I rushed to grab my friend, brought short by the alchemist's iron grip, spinning me about-face.

The parrot, dislodged from Felix in sudden fury, hooked razor claws into flaring nostrils. I took my moment, bristling thorns from my wrist as Fulcanelli swatted the harbinger bird.

"*Puttana ingrata,*" the alchemist cursed. "I'm trying to *save* you!"

Men, I couldn't help the mental eye roll. "Get in line," I shouted, diving into the map.

"Approaching silently, ready to pounce, with fangs bared," the words were shouted after me as I fell away. "The footsteps of a shadow!"

Was *this* what the madman meant?

I saw no shadow — nothing sinister seeming like that, in fact — just an absence. The heart of the man I cared for seemed to still its beat, replaced by the mechanical strokes of a cold blade.

Slash left — an arm flew free. Stab right — a groan and a slump. Not fast enough, though, as Felix kicked the body free and into one raising a rather large axe behind it.

On and on, he danced amidst a whirlwind of violence — face placid, unmoved.

"Felix!!" I cried again, trying to spark some semblance of ration.

Nothing.

Strange creatures with fang-filled mouths roiled forth from the darkness amidst others slightly more human-looking — they weren't, well maybe a couple were, once — to join the assault.

Neither tooth nor claw nor bristle of hair touched Felix in the fray. His luck seemed to still hold sway.

Skill, echoed his love.

Luck is *his greatest skill,* I countered.

Felix's, a quirk of smile, *sure. But* he *has rather more available to him.*

The shred of Dena stitched into my soul wasn't wrong, it seemed. Nothing implausible happened as Felix danced about with the blade. Nothing that would indicate he'd cheated — intentionally or otherwise. And nothing that smacked of the uncanny.

In fact, every eye in this little fae wylde glade was upon him — mine, his attackers', and every bit of *other* that had them to spare though held to the edges — and he seemed in absolutely no hurry to force their collective blink. I'd learned that with that much attention, he *couldn't* cheat.

Not that it particularly mattered any longer as Felix stood amidst the ruin of bodies basking in the light of the forest moon. Steam roiled from his skin in the chill night air. He looked content — sated almost.

He laughed. Rueful, that's how Felix might have described it to you. But that wasn't it. There was no sorrow, no regret — not in that strange soul.

"Is that all you got?"

"Felix?" I quested closer, reaching for my friend.

"The coward's not here right now," not-Felix-then? glared at me. "Please leave a message after the tone." He inverted his grip on the silver sword and struck the blade with a ring that had not been on his finger before — St Germain's, I thought. The clarion sound the weapon made froze the moment in my mind as the world went quiet. Everything held its breath, fearing to draw this killer's attention.

I couldn't blame them. I'd felt the touch of that blade before, I felt certain now.

It was only for a flash, but when the phlogiston flames took my roots in the pit... Felix had done *something* and gone away for a bit after some acrobatics. The pain — excruciating agony, more like — dulled my memory along with the speed of it all, but it rang true in a hollow flash — that was the sword he'd used to cut me free from that unseen hell.

"Well, tell Felix to get his ass back here and explain just what the hell is going on and who the hell you're supposed to be." I wasn't having any of this. I knew he'd had a troubled past, one that gave him nightmares even after the waters of Lethe washed him clean, but this...

"Can't," Felix's face said. "His turn in the cage." He bent, wiping the blade clean on a dead bumper's clothes. I didn't even know what kind it was — Felix always gave me the rundown on who we were dealing with. I missed that.

"What cage? Where *is* he?" I wanted to shake him. For him to tell me it was one of his jokes.

"Ugh," he groaned, stabbing his sword into the ground as he tried to straighten. Ignored. "How does he even fight with this fragile thing?" He kneaded Felix's back and worked out the shoulder. I saw a ripple form from the spine and broaden his shoulders a tiny bit.

"He doesn't." My turn to glare. "Who *are* you?"

"Asher," he cracked his neck.

Fuck.

Double fuck.

Have you ever tried to feel? Like really *tried* to feel something? It's hard.

Impossibly hard.

All the noise. All the doubt. It's so loud all the damn time that true feeling never rises above the din.

At least in my experience.

All my faces displayed emotion — pretty convincingly, if I may be so bold — but they were lies like the rest. Fake.

The rage I currently felt, though, was not. That was so terribly real.

As was the cage I found myself in. One of my own making. Ironic, that.

I slumped to the bars with a forlorn sigh.

"I can't have you roam free," I'd told my dormant self, rendered senseless in the waters of Lethe. "You're a danger," I clanged iron bars into place, "to yourself," I closed the hasp, *and to me.*

The lock, once gleaming silver, had rusted shut with age — rusted *to* the bars. *How'd he get loose?*

The view was beautiful. Endless, almost. I'd allowed myself that much. White fluffy clouds scraped along other peaks capped with snow, giving way to lush greenery. Happy little trees dotted the slopes with squirrels frolicking freely about the branches — or so I imagined.

That's what I'd conjure anyway. Knowing him, the squirrels were probably trying to merc each other for winter stashes and staging epic revenge plots. Maybe that's where the para-wolves had come from, too.

The mountain hadn't been this vibrant, certainly — rather desolate when I'd left my old self behind. Maybe he'd changed as I had, and there were indeed chittering squirrels happily scampering about the boughs of the mountain pines.

He *could* change everything around him save the cell itself — that was immutable.

Supposedly — the fact that I stood here in place of him and he in place of me out there spoke otherwise. The lock was rusted shut, but... I grabbed the bars, each of the thirteen — several wiggled.

Discomforting.

Beyond the bars, the abyss beckoned. Sure, it may look pretty, but it was window dressing — an outlet for sanity to grasp hold — glossing over a chasm in my consciousness.

"There's nothing wrong with having a tree for a friend." Look at Molly.

"One of my favorite Rossisms, dear boy," a figment of memory spoke. "Also partial to: 'Go out on a limb — that's where the fruit is!'"

I sighed. Great, the abyss was talking back.

"How's the dear girl doing?" The words kept flowing as they always had... when he lived. "Did you give her a hug for me, as requested? Maybe you got a little fruit out of it? She's quite enamored of you..."

"Rakozy," I pinched the bridge of my nose. Of course my guilty conscience would taunt me with the remains of St Germain. "Not normal for the dead to talk so much." Restful peace was only proper.

I snuck a peek through the bars to the path just outside, expecting to see the withered, blackened, corrupted husk of the alchemist come to castigate me. But instead, I was met with the bright eyes of the artificer as he'd been before taking the hour from my clock.

"In nature, dead trees are just as normal as live trees." Another Ross.

"And nothing teaches you to hold a knife like a mountain," I pulled one from my ass — the quote, not a knife. "What's it got to do with anything?"

"I've missed you, dear boy," the specter laughed.

"Look," I frowned, "I know what I'm doing."

"Do you really?" St Germain laughed large. "Do enlighten me, I'm so intrigued."

"Manifesting a sore spot in this nothing to throw my concentration from the task at hand with the vain hope of assuaging my guilt with an apology, however hollow it may be," I sighed. "Waste of time," I returned to the wiggling bars, "but the old-school appearance is a nice touch. Thought I'd have gone for the corrupted face bleeding black tears, though."

"Not particularly fond of the desiccated look, dear boy." The figment twirled in his youthful finery.

Frippery might be the better term. He'd not yet developed his minimalist sensibilities and wore a bit of crushed velvet in myriad colors, topping it all off with a blue cap. I don't recall ever having seen him in such, but given his royal roots, I wouldn't be surprised — even before the endless aurum and diamonds, he'd been flush.

"Come to tell me I can just walk out of this jail, too?" I changed the subject back to my confinement.

"This?" St Germain rattled the bars. "Oh no, dear boy. You're well and truly stuck. Can't just waltz out of this one."

"Super helpful," I groaned, knowing he was right. "Thanks."

"Think, though," he continued. "Observe and think. How *did* you get out?"

"That's what I'd like to know." Helpful as it was to have someone other than me to talk things out with, the guilt-ghost wasn't going to offer any solutions I couldn't come to myself. "And what's this all supposed to be?"

"You've seen it before, I'm sure," he was unhelpful. "It'll come to you. Last I saw it, there was a gleaming bridge crossing that river. Very pleasant, until you got pissy."

Briefly, I wondered what river of Avon that was, given where Molly and I'd ended up. So many rivers, so important, all named River. Towers. Bridges. We all fall down.

"But to your earlier inquiry, dear boy," he interrupted. "I do believe other-you's been trying to hang that around your neck," pointing to a darkened corner of the cell where a bloody white heap lay, feathers strewn about.

"The hell's that doing here?" I poked it with my foot, turning the bird over.

Just what my luck needed: a dead albatross.

"Down!" Asher swung for my head.

I dropped, scrabbling backward from the steel — and into the gurgling corpse collapsing behind me. The sword had taken its head — along with a few of my crown leaves.

"Don't *DO* that!" I risked screaming at the guy with a sword. He was still Felix, right? Sort of? *He won't hurt me...right?*

Silence echoed.

"You're welcome," he rolled his eyes, flinging blood from the blade. Blood red as the rest. There'd been no black bile or ichor in the slaughter — no sign of being corrupt. They weren't like the bumpers at the Last Chance. They were still whole.

"Quit *killing* them!" I stalked straight up to his face — nose to nose with the killer. "There's no need."

"That so, cupcake?" He sidestepped me, kicking the body slumped behind me to reveal the dagger in the cold gleam of the moon's light. A dagger that'd have been digging into my kidney had he not swung.

"You didn't have to kill him," I maintained my resolve. "Felix would have found a way."

"Do you have any inkling of what that costs?"

I didn't. He'd just always done it for me.

"Didn't think so," Asher gruffed. "Look, a dead enemy can't stab you in the back tomorrow. Simple as that."

"It's not that cut and dry," I insisted. "Who are they anyway?"

"Doesn't matter."

"Yes it does." I felt like I was arguing with a stump. "If we know who they are and why they're angry, we can get them to stop."

That got a round of laughter inside and out.

"That's rich," Asher gasped for breath. Putting on much?

What's so funny? I asked the echo — she wasn't laughing quite as hard.

"Fucking imbecile," Asher muttered when I didn't join in on the grand joke.

"Excuse me?" I'd about had enough of this fucker — Felix's face or no.

"Not you, cupcake," he waved off my ire. "From what little I've seen, you've a head on your shoulders." Asher cast an appraising eye at me. "Misguided, but a good one."

"Then..."

"*Felix*," he put some stank on it, sheathing his sword. "Keeping you in the deep dark when you're so hell-bent on tagging along. Gutsy." Approval from the murderous asshole — not sure how to feel about that.

"Tell me about it."

He chuckled, taking it as sarcasm. *No, seriously, tell me,* I'd been about to say when an arrow grazed my cheek to land at his feet.

"Don't think I'll have a chance, cupcake." He *schked* his sword clear again, placing himself between me and the rustling forest.

"You're a total badass," St Germain complimented. I'd been checking in on the walking disaster area while trying to swap out, coming upon the battle.

"I assure you, I'm not." I wiggled the bars again, looking for the trick Asher pulled.

"Well, you certainly play several convincingly... Asher there," he nodded, "and what'd you call yourself when..."

"Doesn't matter," I cut him off. I wasn't proud of the things I'd done in some of my lives. Survival isn't always pretty, and those aspects of myself were no longer needed.

"Seems needed to me," the figment of St Germain read my thought. It was a gimme, though.

He'd been watching the melee like a pay-per-view, having a grand old time mimicking my movements as the murderous bastard tore through the onslaught.

"I'd have gotten us out before it came to that," I thought.

"Ah, but you didn't," he countered. He'd gotten a drink from somewhere.

"Thanks to *him*!" I kicked one of the still stout bars.

"It's sad, really," the alchemist sighed. "You two just can't get along."

"You know what happened last time we did," I glared. Wasn't pretty.

"Trivialities," he scoffed.

I glared in a few more languages.

"What? They can make new maps," he laughed. "Gives those stuffy cartographers something to do!"

Sure, what's a measly mountain between friends?

"Oof, good shot boy," St Germain returned to his entertainment. Asher was disemboweling a bumper with cold dispassion.

"Can you not?" The thought of violence grated at me. I'd worked so hard to be clever about it — to leave it behind — and here Asher was stacking bodies.

As soon as that damn skibbity bitch wooped out that pic to the web, I knew... damn internet.

Pics and it happened. Fuck. I needed to think.

"Reminds me of the time in Jabir's little funhouse," the alchemist reminisced.

"I missed one," I grumbled. "Came for me, too. Runty little bastard."

"Ah well, to be expected. Hellacious creatures, those gargoyles. Didn't they rip out that chap's entrails and hang him by them? Oh what was his name? Rob, Robert, Bobert... something," he grimaced. It hadn't been a pleasant dungeon dive, to be sure. "Hope you finished that one off," he made an ick face. "Don't know what Jabir was smoking when he made those."

"Molly didn't want me to," I tested another bar — this one wiggled with a flash of spilled salt.

"Didn't want you to—" St Germain stammered a bit.

"You know how she is with her 'aminals,'" I sighed. The next grasped bar showed me a ladder. I was beginning to see the trick. Clever.

My own fault, too. Never should have broken that damn mirror.

"Named him Gregory," I chuckled. "She was teaching him proper ambush manners. For next time..."

"You named him Gre...? Dear boy," taken aback. "That's all very well and good for you, but what about the poor defenseless Boberts out there?"

"Oh, she made Gregory promise not to hurt anyone else." Nonchalant. I wiggled more bars as Asher rattled the cage of a bumper despite Molly's ire — she was actively getting between them and other-me now. Didn't do too much to save them, though.

"First she curtailed a Bloodybell, now she's tamed a gargoyle," he shook his head.

"Don't forget Tony," I remembered the baby Rokuichi — not so baby anymore. Yeesh.

"Wonder of wonders," he whistled. "Impressive."

"That she is." I felt a bit of pride. She'd taken my life all tipsy-turvy, and I'd have it no other way. Except now, as I watched her face down my killer instinct with... oh shit.

"Oooh ho ho ho ho," St Germain cackled. "Time for the gloves to come off!"

On, in this case, as Molly slid the foxgloves from the twist and up to her wrists.

"Now, now, cupcake," I heard myself say.

Cupcake? "Is he trying to get me punched?"

"You're the one with the silver tongue and touch, dear boy."

"You wanna help me out here before she lays those hands?"

"You'll be fine," he laughed. "Got out before," the alchemist pointed to the me out there, "didn't you?"

"He's had a lot longer to chew on it," I fretted over the scene. What was she going to do with *those*? "And fewer figments distracting him," I shot a side-eye.

"Is that all you think I am, dear boy?" St Germain offended, eyes shifting solely to me. "Some ramshackle figment of your guilty creation?"

"Aren't you?" I didn't have time for the distraction.

"You know what these do." Molly flexed her threatening fingers — the supple green leather fitting like a second skin. Pink-tipped fingers came eagerly close.

"Damnit, Rakozy," I mildly panicked. "Would you quit being so damn dramatic while I'm trying to save my skin here?"

"G'head," he waved. "Do your thing. Asher's better company anyway." He vanished before I could even process *that.*

"I do," other-me confirmed. *"Do you? Or just what Felix said they did? Two different things."*

Doubt flashed across her face. I did have a point there.

"I know I've used them to rip a soul apart," she countered, her words whispering through the leaves. *"Like what needs doing here, I think."* Smart girl.

"I wish you hadn't said that," my other's tone turned dark. *"Felix is rather fond of you, but..."* Asher took a guard stance.

"I've no such attachment holding you safe," Asher raised his sword against me.

I swallowed and stood my ground. He was bluffing.

At the edge of notice, I heard the brush bristle and shift at the passing of small feet. Great. *What's next?*

Keep him distracted, the echo in my heart.

"You're a terrible person." Verbal assault it was.

"I've been told," Asher held his ground. "Matters not."

"It does, too. Kindness costs nothing, you know."

Wrong thing to say, I realized as his face darkened — any lightness left replaced by deepening shadow.

"Kindness," he spat. "Kindness cost me *everything.*" He lunged, striking for me true.

I tumbled backward, scrabbling away as he stabbed the ground at my feet.

"Ask Dena what kindness cost her," he stalked closer. "Ask why the Bloodybell exacts his price," he stabbed the ground again. *"A kindness if ye please,"* he mocked with another jab.

Horrible. How could he feel that way?

"*They* come hat in hand wanting and thieving and stealing — greed and unslaked bloodlust. All of them." Murder in his eyes. Murder I'd seen before through the eyes of another.

"You're the one who killed the gargoyles," I disconnected. "Not Felix." He'd taken the blame for it, but now it made sense when I saw this cold-hearted killer. My heart hurt for him.

"The monsters needed killing, and I do what's necessary." Was this monster truly who Felix had been, before? How could he be so warped and broken?

Wasn't always, the echo in my soul. *The crucible of life is unkind.*

"That's *why* we need kindness," I answered the voice in my head aloud.

"Excuse me?" Lightning flashed.

"You heard me," I pressed. "The world is cruel enough. Survival is one thing — you do what you gotta do." I risked a step closer, taking the gloves off. "But you're better than this." *My* Felix was, at least. "Time and time again, you've proved it."

"I fail where it matters most. Ironically," this time the laugh *was* rueful, "without fail."

"You're not a failure," I smacked him. "Quit saying that kinda shit with his face."

Lightning flashed as an owl ghosted overhead. Quick as that, he came closer...

...and kissed her. After everything she said, I could, and did.

"Thanks for sticking up for me, Molls." She smacked me again.

"Don't call me Mol... Felix?" She jumped in my arms, wrapping hers around my neck — gloves brushing me briefly.

"Careful with those," I cringed at their touch. Less potent than when worn, they still burned one like me.

She sprang away from me. "How?"

"There was this albatross and an alchemist," I started. "Good show, by the way. Proud of you," I smiled. "Standing your ground like that."

"Would it have worked?" She fell for the tangent. "I thought maybe I could do that soul-taffy thing I did with Deirdre."

"It'd have killed me," I said. "Straight up. No taffy."

"Oh, well that won't do." Anger, concern, sadness — all mixed and mingled on her face.

"Will if it needs to," I got serious. "I've got him locked up pretty tight, but if it comes to that — do it." I didn't trust myself to not get out again. I didn't say, *I'll be fine.*

"He said it was your turn in the cage." Molly's eyes held a thousand questions — I needed to be better about their answers.

"Funny thing about cages — sometimes they protect the world at large from what's inside." My senses prickled. "Sometimes, the opposite," I pulled Molly behind me. "You never turn the light on in a dark room."

Lightning flashed a third time.

We were surrounded. Too many eyes blinking out of sync.

"Just might see what's there." I kinda wished for that sword now. Hissing and spitting, the not-a-foxes surrounded us. "Put the gloves on."

"No need, my love," Molly's voice deepened. "They're here for me."

"Dena?" I turned, my heart stopping a beat. Molly's willowy hazel had been replaced by emeralds.

"For a moment more," she sighed, kissing me herself.

I felt the too-many eyes of the creatures all around me. They'd never actually liked me — who had really? — but they listened to her. Mostly.

"Be careful love," she cupped my cheek. "Your shadow walks faster than you," she warned and faded — the too-many eyes around us winking out.

Tell me something I don't know.

The gemstones faded to a more verdant shade as Molly came to the fore.

"Let's go home," I said, her hand still cupping my face.

"But how? We've been turned around for days."

"Easy," I grinned. "I know where we are now." Visited Nemli lots of times. His cabin... "Well shit." ...was on fire.

"Someone's gonna be pissed," Molly stood extra close to me.

I sighed — both frustrated and content.

Knights of the Holey Pail

"I'VE HEARD OF GETTING lost in a book, but that's preposterous." Marty unshelved another book that smelled of almonds — *For Whom the Bell Tolls* — infected like so many others.

"Most of it really happened," I protested for form's sake, following.

Elliot, for his part, declined to weigh in on the subject. His only concern was that I'd retrieved such a pristine incunabulum — as he called the unwritten book — for him. Guess it sounds fancier, like all medicines.

Witchcraft, all of it — then and now — talking in code like the bloody alchemists and their jibberish. Science, they call it now. The *language of birds* they called it then. Same cryptic bullhockey — no different than what Jabir wrote all his instructions in — yeah, guy that made the gargoyles. Him. Really glad that asshole never took any elixir — one lifetime was bad enough for him.

Now, he had good reason for the nonsense — people historically haven't taken too kindly to those trucking with powers beyond mortal ken, still don't. Lots of unkind bonfires and such.

To be honest, some of it didn't help their case — calling mustard seeds 'eye of newt' and buttercups 'toe of frog' and the like. Gave people the heebs. "Got any wool of bat handy?" I'd non-sequitured to Molly once. She had no clue what I was on about. Means holly leaves, by the way. I'd been Christmas crafting — much to her dismay. Or moss.

I like moss. So soft and comforting. Cool in the summer and can keep a cabin warm in the winter. Much better than bonfires.

Or books being burned, I snapped back to Lenore's quarantine section.

"Just sorry the monks weren't there to fix the infected ones." It'd been a total cluster at the bottom of that labyrinth even before Fulcanelli put one over on me.

Things hadn't been too much better here, if the alcove of the infested was any indication. Marty'd been busy while we were gone — going through Elliot's entire hoard, pulling out the nesting imps. At least now the unwritten book sat open on the shelves — marginalia snails just waiting to snap up the greedy imps.

It wasn't as quick as the blind scribes' brute force extermination, but it should work. Would be a shame to lose all the infected. Lots of classics and more modern tales. I came across one in particular that tugged at me.

"Sorry, Felix." Marty looked over his readers, seeing where my finger had landed when I sighed — one of mine.

"Probably made it better," I laughed. "Besides, who could tell the difference anyway? Up the antics, I say."

I say a lot of things, though. Like: "I make most of this shit up as I go," I assured Marty. Names are changed to protect the guilty, yadda-yadda.

Elliot brushed up against my leg, acting much more cat than dragon.

"They're meant to be an escape and so long as people can pass through the pages, who really cares?" Best place to get lost is in a book.

"Like when you escaped the... Scriptorum, you called it?" That's what everyone called it 'cause that's what it's called.

"Yes, exactly!" I was surprised Marty had never heard of the place before, given his familiar relationship with Elliot. "I'm sure you've been there," I addressed the dragon in the room.

"Right," Marty elongated, exchanging a look with the cat.

"You have any Polish dictionaries?" I asked on a whim. "Or encyclopedias." It'd be amusing to see one of those imp-infested — they were already brilliantly absurd.

"Fresh out," he worried.

"Bummer, they have the best definition of horse." I laughed a few threads loose. "*Everyone can see what a horse is,*" I intoned the mock. "Great one for *dragons*, too," I glanced at Elliot and wandered off to search.

I wasn't quite sure the dragon-cat was actually on my side anymore. Not after that fool's errand. *Is anyone, though?* Had he known?

That's what the midnight voices told me anyway. You know, the ones who whisper in the mist of dreams you can't quiet remember — the real ones that feel. The doubts that gnaw. The scribbled brilliance that looses luster by light of day.

Molly had left me. That was a surprise.

Skedaddled right when we got back. I guessed she needed some time to herself — said she had to check in with Hank. Make sure the Last Chance wasn't in shambled disrepair.

It was what I wanted, wasn't it? Get her away from my splash-zone, so maybe she didn't get caught up in my ever-growing mess.

The key in my pocket grew heavy. Entirely useless in the fae wylde, that iron key. Far too removed from supposed civilization to have any back rooms or alleys become forgotten. Rabbit trails, sure. The odd secret garden, definitely.

That's how we'd gotten back — took the upright door left down in the woods. One forgotten by he who built it back in the day. The house gone to ruin, tumbled down around it and rotted — yet the polished cherry door remained. Kids, don't try that at home — going through strange doorways when you can see the other side. Or those creepy stairs in the middle of the forest — you really don't want to know where *those* go. And it's not anywhere close to what you think.

Trust me. You won't like it.

"Felix?" Marty called me where I wasn't.

The key in my pocket grew hot now, bumping and banging against my leg. Definitely time to go.

"Over in reference," I threw my voice atta-way. I liked Marty, I did. Been good to me when I had no idea who I was. Real good. Letting me lose myself in page after page.

But neither he nor Elliot wanted trouble — and that's just what I was of late. Probably to blame for their impish misfortune, to boot — I wondered how many of those afflicted my mind had wandered through. Unsettling tangent.

Who'd blame them for dropping a dime on me once I came back 'round? Not me. Not with the price still on my head and lots of, well, not-quite-people after me. Elliot had the misfortune of being seen with me at the ball, and who knew who'd paid the shop a visit after.

I couldn't slip out in the twist — Elliot was too aware for that — but the key could take me lots of places.

Trouble was, where to?

"He kissed me!" I couldn't believe he just up and kissed me like that. That was *not* how I pictured it at all. I threw back a shot and poured another.

"At the ball would have been perfect, if it weren't for all the psychos — though the danger might have added a little something to it," I rambled on to Elder as he drank lager straight from the barrel.

"No, of course he'd kiss me right as I'd decided to kill him." Hadn't been an easy decision. "Frankly, I thought it was a delay tactic," I sulked slightly. I'd have tried to enjoy it otherwise. Asshole.

"Boy's timing sucks," Hank nosed in. "You think'd be better, having all of it and what-not."

I took another shot. Didn't want to think about that part. His past self *was* the problem. But I needed to know.

"Who's Asher?" I slid liquid bribe to Hank.

The old devil straight up spat — bluthering and hundering as he threw back the offering with a skyah.

"Where the blazes you hear that name, missy?" Hank gripped his mangled hand into a bloodless fist. Obviously not a fan.

"I think I met him," I soured myself. "Earlier."

"Ought to be rotting away in Gehenna's dumps, that one," he spat again for good measure.

"But he's still Felix, right?" This part still hurt my head — and no small part my heart, if... "Part of him?"

"Bad part," Hank undersold. "We got problems if he's cutting loose." Hank looked near to murder. "Is he?"

"Still to be determined," I pulled my best Magic 8-ball. Good ol' floaty D20 in blue goop — that reel had tickled a switch in the memory banks, never to be forgotten. "But I think Felix put a lid on it." Unless he was faking — I couldn't entirely be sure. And that bothered me.

He'd never given me reason to doubt. Sure, Felix was a con artist, profligate liar, and only said a sliver of what he meant — but he was honest about it. Game recognizes game, so even when he was bullshitting me, I *knew* he was doing it, and he knew I knew. If that makes any nonsense.

Asher was... different. Cold, lacking, not all there.

"You sure about that?" One bushy brow rose.

Not really, I didn't say, my body language twisting for a change of tack.

Hank hnged at the diverted silence, taking it for answer enough. I could see the gears turning in the old devil's mind.

"I don't like him," Hank gruffed and grimmed. "No good."

"In the bed, though," another voice joined in, eyebrows raised a bit. "Oh! I knew him when," Deirdre joined the merry little chat — actually I think Zestra was signed on. "Let me tell you," the medium's eyebrows arched suggestively.

"Ew." I blushed for Deirdre's sake. Mine, too. Inside, the echo blushed in memory. Horny jail, the lot of you. "Also, elaborate — not on the carnal parts."

"Why skip the good parts, honey?" The dead gypsy gyrated a bit with a smile. "But if you must. Yes, he is dangerous. Very dangerous. I don't need my crystal ball to tell you that."

Could've told her that.

"The man walked willingly through death's door," Zestra said. "Twice, at least. How many do that?"

"You mean he killed himself?" The thought sickened me.

"No," Zestra said. "Much more complicated for him, I think. I first met him in the land of the dead, you know? But he came back."

"Does that." Hank took another drink.

"How?" Seemed kind of important.

"Gooood question." Hank offered no answer. "Have to ask him."

Zestra shrugged Deirdre's shoulders. Funny thing, since I'd worn the gloves, I could see her... just a little bit. See more of the *other* things in the world.

"Felix told me to... you know," I blurted. "If it came to that."

"Ha!" Hank wobbled back with the laugh. "Good luck, missy."

I shot the old devil a look.

"Can't," he drank his reply. "Lots tried. Never sticks."

See a penny, pick it up, I hummed to myself, spying shiny copper other side of the door I'd just opened. Could use some good luck of late.

Prepare all you can, you just know it's all going to change. Especially when someone swings a sword at you the second you step through.

On borrowed instinct, I ducked lest my head be quacked open. Get it?

"Should've died when you had the chance!" A second attacker leapt from the dumpster across the alley from me, brandishing a sword.

"What's with that line?" I rolled to the side as the first tried a pommel strike. The toady wizard had shouted it too, I vaguely recalled. Was it requisite to collect the bounty? Was this Candid Camera? Or Punk'd? Whatever the new prank show was — I'd have to ask Molly, I'm sure it was on an app somewhere.

Provided these chumps didn't skewer me first. Normally, I wouldn't give it a second thought. They'd just bonk into each other and crumple back into the bin like the garbage knights they were — but *someone* was mucking about.

"On guard, vile fiends." I brazenly grabbed a discarded pipe, waving the rusted end in their faces. "Have at ye," I laughed. This shit never happened.

I mean, seriously. Who gets accosted by a couple loons wearing armor — and I'm being generous with that word. One wore a gleaming trash can hiked up to the waist, hung by a bit of rope. The other wore bulbous silver plate with a small bucket on his head — couple holes cut out to see. The first had a bent mixing bowl strapped under white-whiskered chin, tinted visor raised.

Like some grown-up kids playing knights and goblins, using the can lids for shields. Those at least made sense — being round with a handle for holding, only natural. I'd used them as such myself. Their swords, I half expected to be cardboard tubes.

Disappointingly, they were actually gleaming sharp steel — even in the dark of the alley they shone bright, sending my shadow dancing.

"Have at we?!?" Whiskers sputtered, outraged. "You're the vile fiend here... fiend!" Clever wordplay, that.

I giggled. In all his sputtering, his makeshift visor — scrounged from a motorcycle helmet, I think — fell down.

"Laugh in the face of justice, will you?" I couldn't help it. They'd gotten the drop on me, sure, but it seemed their backup plan was to split my sides another way.

"Stop! Stop, you're killing me with the bit." I wiped tears from my eyes, steel pipe clanging to the cracked asphalt of the alley.

"Then you yield?" The smug satisfaction on the garbage knight's face irked me.

"No," I chuckled, "but you've got a killer routine. Reminds me a bit of Python." I casually walked up to the one not struggling to climb out of the dumpster — the big one. The one who wasn't all blunder and buss — that one hadn't said a damn word. "Where're your coconuts?" I tried to peer under the lunch pail on the fella's head.

The knight swung a broad arc; I ducked.

Tried next for an overhand, I swatted it with the back of my hand — blade harmlessly striking sparks against brick.

A grin spread under the tin can, grinding steel along the wall like a match til it struck aflame. This one was getting ideas.

I gleed just a bit — might be a bit of a challenge. I cracked my neck. *No!* — Asher was bleeding through.

Still, I flexed my hand, aching for a proper blade. In its stead, I toe-flipped the pipe I'd dropped back into my grasp — better than *that* blade drawn again.

Achoo. Fuck.

"For all these tents and porpoises, eh?" Wow, that accent was thick — couldn't quite place the borough. Been a minute since I'd darkened the Big Apple, but I was pretty sure Ez B'd pulled that one out his ass for nonsensical grandiloquence.

"Tushy," he laughed, smacking the big one on said point of contact. "Boy, you came in at the wrong time," he turned his attention to me, "for you anyway."

"I arrive precisely when I intend," I misquoted. "Neither early, nor late."

"Yer not a wizard, dear foe," he mocked, reminding me where I still stood.

"What'd ya mean 'for me'?" Ez B was up to something, but least the garbage knights hadn't pressed. Meaning I could squash Asher's violent upwelling.

"Well, for my operational smoothness, it's absolutely perfect timing," he grinned. "For your sanity, terrible."

Whiskers huffed up at that. "But... the posters said..."

"Consider them suspended under eggsbenedict circumstances," he turned on the pair. I cleared my ear — that hadn't been an accent thickening. And what posters?

"How about you try making some sense?" I knew it didn't come naturally to the bastion of the back alleys, but was only courteous when one asks for help — as it seemed he was about to. He hadn't called his dogs off for not.

"Where's the fun in that, dear foe?" He jabbed at me with his stank finger — I think he'd ripened it even more since I'd last seen him. He really didn't like me — or Asher, one.

"I don't think anyone's having any sort of fun with any bit of this, least of all me," I grumped. "Especially with Humpty and Dumpty trying to clean my clock soon as I stepped foot." I couldn't think of a pairing for Whiskers, thus the renaming. He was Dumpty, for obvious reasons. "What's with the tin cans anyway?"

"Things getting a bit scritchy," he scratched his nose. "Set some guard posts."

Ez B nodded the pair back into begrudging place as I passed.

"Ran out of armor, I see." Upon closer inspection, Humpty's broad shoulders were laundry bottles painted silver. "But damn fine swords."

"Strongest steel is forged in the fires," he flared a bit dramatic, "of a dumpster," he kicked said blue bin.

Achoo.

I seconded the sneeze — the scent of garbage fires tickling my nostrils, attention now drawn to it. The back alleys were chillier than they should have been — wasn't even Halloween yet.

"Get to it." I didn't have time for this. "What's got you asking favors?"

"No favor has been asked," Ez B splashed a puddle. "Do you offer?"

"Sure don't," I stepped to the side, looking for that penny I'd spied earlier. "But you're angling for one."

"That's a brilliant idea!" The madman clicked his heels in a jump. "Marvelous, really." He pulled a collapsible rod from his pocket and clapped my shoulder.

"You want to go fishing?" Copper winked at me. Snatch.

"Something like that," he set off, whistling.

Tails. Damn.

"That's absurd!" Preposterous, really.

"How it goes," Hank nodded.

"And you're okay with that?" I couldn't believe it.

"'Course not!" Hank's face scrunched. "Who would be? But I don't see as we got much of a choice," he settled his arms across his chest.

"There's always a choice!" I wouldn't let him.

"Sure, missy," he agreed. "Just not always ours. 'Sides, he owes me favors three."

"So he'll just up and die if you tell him to?" Circle back to absurd here.

"Not as such," Hank scratched his eye. "He's tricksy."

"I'm aware," I flattened my voice. Oh, how I was aware.

"But yeah, boils down to that."

"And he'll just let you ask him? If it's Asher run amok won't he just..." I drew my thumb across my throat making a kgckk sound.

"Prolly kill me on the spot," Hank admitted, draining a glass. "Won't chance it," he chuckled, flexing his mangled hand. "Get it?"

"Yeah, and we're back to no!" It'd been the best plan we'd had over the three emptied bottles but it still sucked. "Do me a favor and think a'something better!"

"What'd ya say, missy?" The old devil squinted — I could see rust-seized gears cranking.

"Do me a..." Favor! "Hank... tell me about these *favors*."

"Yoink!" Ez B tugged his prize through the sewer grate.

"Huzzah! You caught soggy shoe leather," I rolled my eyes.

"Dinner," the sneezing man grinned, setting it on the pavement.

"Oooh! Fillet of soul? Bet the leather's nice and tender. Lots of flavorful penicillin, to boot." My puns had the decency to be intended.

"Ye of absent faith," he tsked as the boot started to squishily flop. "Have a see."

"Fuck me." There *was* a fish in the boot.

"No thanks," Ez B declined. "That's all you, boo. No need to drudge up the past."

"Hut tut, what have we now?" A voice from nowhere. "Yer not supposed to be fishing these waters, dumplins," the voice straggled. Bile stench crawled up my nostrils as I turned to meet inky black eyes shining through lank hair nattier than a rat's nest. "Those tales be mine for the tasting, they be."

Bibliophage, the word whispered to me.

I cringed as if something slurped my neck. The form before me — bent and broken, prickly twisted with spines — splayed arms akimbo as it swayed down from above, lascivious tongue tasting the air for book pages.

"Unequivocably!" Ez B dumped the boot and drew the creature's attention as I stood stock still — proffered fish tale flopping about the pavement.

Fear froze me in front of the phage — my feet wont to move lest I draw those devouring eyes, now fixed on the fish unraveling into ether. My skin crawled in sympathy for the fish — its existence surrendered.

"*Now,*" the sneezing man whispered, quite urgent. "Do your thing," he elbowed me from stupor.

My thing? Brain froze in fight or flight conflation. Time stretched like a gummy.

Of all the things I'd forgotten in the waters of Lethe, the phages were not one — they still gave me nightmares as did their cousins, the vore. Some terrors can never be washed clean — seared into the very molecules of grey matter mushing about one's skull. Phages were such, an existential threat of the highest magnitude — confabulations cultivated in an ersatz world.

But, they liked the shiny and therein lie they're weekness. I stealed my resolve as words went wonk in the presence of their unmaking. A book bound in elegant crystal grown — imp infection sealed in time, an original Wonderland, gone too far.

"MINES," the bibliophage veritably leapt to lap at my hand, licking the bejeweled tome, taking the poison most willfully.

My hand burned to the touch and I think I left my consciousness behind as the phage closed on me — body acting soully in self-preservation.

My shadow sliced as the bibliophage gacked, inky eyes bulging and burst.

My head pounded, threat subdued.

I spun on the sneezing man come to see the phage's diaphanous demise, slamming him into crumbling back alley brick.

"Are you actively trying to kill me?" My mind flowed back from the edges to which it had fled, collecting happenstance and adding up the 'dear foes' dropped along the way.

"Asher again, are we?" He gripped my shadow's hand as it fixed him in place — I hadn't moved, it would seem. My own hands empty, though the one not pinning the shit-stank man curled as if around the hilt of a sword — one visibly held by my shadow.

"No," I didn't think. I'd acted out of self-preservation. "I can get him if you like." I put on my sharpest smile. A smile I remembered smiling in lives long past. A smile I never liked all that much, but which had its place — like now. My shadow leaned in.

"Best not," he tapped out. I let him drop. "Had enough monsters for one day."

Ouch.

"What'd you do?" He toed the crystal tome, laying empty now that the phage had supped.

"What you asked," I kept it simple. "And so politely, I might add."

"Would you've helped if I hadn't had your feet to the fire?"

"Of course," I lied. Like hell I'd take on any sort of phage by choice — biblio-, grammo-, logo-. I shuddered at the last one. I wanted fuckall to do with anything that ate legend and lore.

I fiddled with the ring on my pinky — it was new to me and sat uncomfortably. I wasn't sure where it'd come from, only that it was there when I'd come to after the woods. Garish in gold and amber, I'd seen him wear it many a time, never noticing the cameo etched inside — the spitting image of Rakozy as I'd just imagined his figment.

As I caught his specter's eye, the Compte de St Germain winked.

"You wanna know?" Hank waggled his eyebrow. "I'll give you a guess: only word that has three double letters all squished up together," he crossed his arms. He'd been less than keen on the notion of me taking over one of his favors.

I wasn't exactly keen on it myself, but it was the best of a bunch of bad options — always look for the bright spot. Felix taught me that. The thought of going up against him — well, Asher wearing his face (totally rude) — soured me.

"There we go sweetie," Ruth closed her ledger — registering the favor to me.

Bookkeeper, by the way. That was the answer. Easy riddle to get distracted on — I kept thinking of states like Mississippi and Tennessee. Vowels getting in the way.

"Eighteen left of 195," Ruth said unbidden.

"That seems pretty favorable." I had no idea, but wanted to be positive.

"Better than it could be, certainly, sweetie," she laughed. "He has a way with that." Her smile lingered for a moment. "But it still ends in one. You just sealed it." The Remembrancer — that's what Felix called her, right? Fancy name for accountant-slash-bookkeeper — patted the ledger.

I'd been confused when I figured out Hank's riddle — what did Ruth have to do with favors? She collected rent, right?

Turns out she collects on *all* debts.

"One is better than none," I borrowed a bit of Deirdre's near-constant cheer. *I'd make it be.*

Ruth smiled bigger, eyes lighting a little mysteriously. I felt a little swirly looking at them as if suddenly on a shifting boat.

"It certainly is, sweetie," she patted my arm. "It certainly is. Now, let's get you fed," ever ebullient. No wonder Felix called her his favorite aunty. "You're thin as a twig!"

Death Rides
a Pale
Lawnmower

"THEY'RE ALL DEAD NOW," I slid a ribbon toward Damian. I'd been telling him exactly how real unicorns were. Past tense, thank goodness.

Weird how we'd gotten on the subject — traumatic eighties movies for a thousand, Alex — but he bet they did exist.

"Man, I don't believe half the shit you tell me," he laughed, "and usually it costs." Still a skeptic, he'd become way more open to *other* than I'd ever had thought — thanks to our friendly wagers, I'd like to think.

Kept me pretty flush, that's for sure. I liked that about Damian — always honored his end of a bet. Not my fault he didn't know it was a losing one. I can usually back my big mouth.

"Well, this time I'm telling you upfront," I straightened non-existent lapels. "Right noble, I'd say."

"So what is this then?" He put his beer down and picked up the ribbon. If it wasn't so damn dark in here, he'd see it was uncharacteristically fancy. Thread of gold trimmed the edges of the red ribbon in archaic designs — nearly too fine to see.

Definitely too fine to see at the bar — what the hell was it that associated dim lighting with 'atmosphere' anyway? Probably a fae trick, that. Started so prospective entres couldn't get a good look at the sharp teeth before being tucked into.

"Proof." Half-true, but Damian didn't need to know that. Was actually my last unicorn ward — well, tourniquet — against the parasites, but they were extinct now, hallelujah. Right horrid bastards really — burrowing deep into the equine brain to take control and feed — like those zombie ants. Carnivorous fungus, really. Dreadful.

"That unicorns existed?" Damian examined the ribbon as closely as he could. "How?"

"Exciting!" This from Berlyn — yes with a 'y' for reasons known only to her mother — freshly freshened up in the loo. Technically, her name was Chamberlyn — too many fantasy novels was my guess. She was around the age that'd be seriously cringe if Damian hadn't introduced her as his niece.

In fact, she'd wanted to have drinks with Sassy-pants for her twenty-first birthday present, but he'd been unable to make it. So here I was, second- or third-best option. Yay.

"It could be from some knight's favor or a medal of valor," she glommed onto the idea. "For killing the last one," she considered between squees. Ah youth — I wasn't the only one falling into books. "Is it a charm?"

"Quite," I admired. "Wear it tied in your hair," I instructed. "And if anyone's suspicious or makes you uncomfortable, just tug," I mimicked, "and they'll vanish."

For theatrical purposes, I did just that — appearing behind Berlyn with a fresh beer for her and a wink for Damian — woe be unto anyone who messed with this girl. "Happy twenty-one!"

"That's so cool!" She took the beer and clanked, taking a sip of her first drink.

Make that a chug, followed by a slammed pint and a burp. "Ugh, that's piss beer." She turned to the bartender.

"Martini, blue cheese olives," she ordered. "Make it dirty," she added, flashing cash.

Okay, first *legal* drink, I quirked my thought. Damian just kinda said nothing, frozen halfway through his beer.

"What?" Berlyn caught the look pass between me and Damian.

"Well, she *is* your niece," I laughed.

I really wasn't sure how I'd gotten there — no, I wasn't drunk. But in a general sense, the trail of coincidence and synchronicity leading to crashing a friend's niece's twenty-first birthday party was pretty, well...

Here's what happened.

After the sneezing man pressed me into exterminatorial services — cleaning up the back alley pest — I wanted nothing to do with the *other* side of the street for a bit and decided to try having a quote-unquote *normal* day.

Should've known it'd get me in deeper.

I mean, look at what happened the *last* time I tried to get soup.

Sigh. I missed Molly.

It started off nice enough — taking a little day trip out to Stoney Meadows — despite her absence. I'd be lying if I said I wasn't worried about her, but I lie a lot. She was a big girl, quite capable. She had help beside me — heavy hitters, too. She'd be fine.

I wasn't worried. Except maybe she'd kill me for going without her, but... she had her reasons.

And I wasn't going to worry about the bombshells Ez B had dropped on me in the back alleys like so many trebucheted pumpkins.

Now Emmett, he worried me. Most of the folk at Stoney Meadows, too. He'd missed out on punkin chunkin this year — highly unlike the tinkerer.

NO PROPANE, EMMETT!!!

The signs had been hung by the entrance with care, but the rascally old coot, he just wasn't there.

The punkins were chunked, their guts strewn the field, very well spread. Feed for the critters against winter's dread.

Ahem, anyway. They'd set up the farm for Christmas — which was totally why I wasn't too worried about Molly getting mad at me; she hated that shit. Jingles jangled and stuff found stockings. General merriment ensued amongst the Frasers and the Dougs laid out with care.

The farm had been nice, and I'd avoided any untoward encounters or having adventure thrust upon me. Excellent.

I was tired of doing main character shit, so I'd decided to lose myself for a bit with some of that psychogeography stuff I'd told Molly about. Needed to think about some good rules, though. Couldn't trust passing cats or bats or any animals really — talk about cahoots — and third lefts always make a right, so instead, I made a paper airplane from a parking ticket.

Sorry George, I'm sure it'll work out for you, whoever you are. There were three under the wiper of the Buick as it was — more surprised he hadn't gotten booted. Yet. Maybe they boot it at the fourth? You're welcome, George.

The idea was simple enough — six throws and there I'd go. See the what's what and decide if something shiny caught my eye. Take the normal streets — no back alleys or twisted paths, just good, honest footwork.

The first throw had landed in a bush — a wayward yew, escaped from the cemetery with its berries so red — inauspicious start, for sure. At least it wasn't thorny as I retrieved the haphazard plane.

Second, nothing much to report, landing in an unused loading zone with a yellow curb. Third, much the same, but under a car — Mazda, for those who wondered.

The fourth landed in a baby carriage — thankfully parked at the park, the mother and child off to play. Trying not to call attention to myself here, thank you very much.

The fifth I launched pretty hard and it stuck up in a tree. Maple, I think, no relation to Molly. Branches entirely bare at this chilly juncture in the year gone awry — where the hell had summer gone with fall coming out of season? Now winter loomed large. It bothered me, needed to look into that at some point. But not now — I had enough going on, also thank you *very* much.

When did everyone else's problems become mine? Was I really the adultiest adult now by virtue of attrition? Thoughts drifted dark, I shook my head. Fuck that noise.

All these thoughts tumbled through my head as I climbed higher and higher, the plane having ridden a gust of wind up and up beyond where its slipshod design should allow. Reaching the maple's crown, I retrieved the airplane and found no need for a sixth throw.

I threw it anyway, perfunctorily — the parking ticket plane confirming my destination as it slid under the patient's bed, unaware.

"I'll have you know that fat does a body good," the man patted his belly. "Helps the recovery, it does."

"And I'm sure the padding's helped a time or two," the nurse chuckled, dropping eaves on the phone call.

"That it has, that it has." The missing Emmett waved the futzy nurse out. "But green beans *not* cooked in bacon grease? That's a downright crime!"

I heard bits from the other side of the phone — being up extra loud to accommodate a lifetime of booms — but I couldn't quite catch it all.

"The lard works in mysterious ways." I hopped from tree to sill after the nurse had skedaddled — winking at Emmett. It seemed a look of surprise crept over his face as I landed. Hard to tell — the pyroenthusiast's eyebrows were still missing.

"Hey, I've gotta go," the old man paused. "There's a caped man in my window." What cape? I checked behind me.

"Oh, I'm sure it's nothing," I heard through the phone, though I doubt Emmett did. "They give you the good shit?" Laughter came across just as he cut it.

"The hell's your window doing open in winter, man?" I hopped into the room. "Wanna catch your death?"

It wasn't exactly a hospital, more a recovery ward, unless I missed my guess. I didn't see a handy-dandy name tag on the building as I was tossing the airplane. Er, I mean sign. Street numbers are all well and good, but it helps to know the names of places just like with people.

"That why you've come?" Emmett swallowed hard, sweat beading on his naked brow. "Come to collect my soul?" Terrified.

Of me?

"Who what now?" I tried for calm, slightly confused. "Sorry to startle you like that." Damn fool, dropping in on an old guy from the damn window. Of course I'd scared him. "Definitely not here to hurt you," cause that's what not-murderers say. "It's Felix. From punkin chunkin?"

No good. He cringed back as I stepped closer, clutching the blanket closer as my shadow stretched toward him.

"Aaaaahhhh..." he squeaked, a near soundless vocalization I felt more than heard as I realized I hadn't moved...

But my shadow had.

Shit. I dove for the door, trying to put the light between me and Emmett to cast my shadow back. I felt it now, dripping from my shoulders, inky and puddling at my feet. Tripping me into a tumble against the wall, grabbing for something to break it.

I flopped about like a prat as my shadow grew. Somehow, in the discomboble, my hand landed on an umbrella by Emmett's door, triggering the mechanism to spring it open inside.

Great. Just great — another bit of luck eroded away.

Sudden as a storm, the pressure in my head vanished — shadow subsiding once more to only that cast by light.

"You said you'd come for it," Emmett hid. "Said I had one. Most don't. I'd know by your shadow, you said." He rocked in the bed, risking a look as he kept repeating the words.

I risked one, too. Just a peek. It made sense — Emmett certainly sparked with vivacity. The world was full of Hylics, but Emmett was not one. He did indeed have a soul, I saw, judging by the hazy blue flame coursing through his being. Fortunate — not many got one anymore. Full one anyway.

"Shhh, shhh," I stood. "I haven't come for nothing," I assured. "What's yours is yours and I've no right to take it."

"You said you'd come for it," he repeated, eyes in distant memory. "Said when you pulled me from the ice," he shivered.

"Ice?" I sat gently in the chair next to him, careful not to let my shadow cross his. Sometimes it was easier to talk through the memory than against.

"We were out fishing, you and me," Emmett recalled. "River'd frozen over good — had to use a chainsaw on the ice — and boy, we were freezing our nutsacks off," he slipped back in time.

I had no memory of this. As far as I knew, I'd just met the tinkerer at the last Pumpkin Brawl when he chased me and Molly down with his Fall Guy truck.

"Damn moose bowled us over and stole our six-pack," he surled. "Sent me sprawlin' into the hole. Should'a died then," eyes grown distant, he went on, "but you said no. Sent your shadow to pull my ass out."

I didn't press. Must've been a horrible thing for him — had some experience with that myself.

"Said it'd be a shame to cut this one short," he patted his heart. "Let it go to waste when there hadn't been too many people to get a soul for a while. Make the most of it, you said."

"Not wrong about that," I agreed. They were in dreadfully short supply after I was born — the first time — capping out around half a billion, give or take a country.

See, the stuff to make 'em was running out faster than people were being born — more and more were getting the short end of that particular stick. Decisions were made.

Reduce. Reuse. Recycle.

Emmett had calmed a bit as he'd talked and my shadow behaved.

"You some kind of angel?" He guessed wrong. "Never saw you before and didn't see you after. Just saved my ass, said some batshit, and left."

Sure sounded like my M.O.

"I think I'm ready," he steeled himself — waiting for some sort of scythe to swing. "Got a sign earlier."

"You know, the reaper doesn't carry a scythe to harvest people," I tangented. "Not all that grim, either." Walked with him a couple times, myself. Good company. Likes games.

"Why then?" Emmett followed along.

"Same as anyone else," I met his clearing eyes. "Cut the grass."

"Cut the grass?" Berlyn looked slightly underwhelmed, turning her attention to the skates she was lacing.

I thought it was a great punchline, but maybe she'd wanted more of a zing. I hadn't told them about Emmett — that was private, too close to home. Had a nice long chat, though — but the reaper bit was prime material. Though, on second thought, I should be careful before Damian wanted to have a drink with death. Currently, he was inspecting a horse for unicorn polyps.

"Yeah," I hedged a bit, "path to heaven isn't used much anymore. Gets overgrown." I laced up my own. Who even knows how we got from the bar to the ice skating rink, excepting that we did. That's how life goes, you know —

"Doesn't death have a lawnmower?" The question seemed vapid, but these kids today also thought phones were shaped more like PopTarts than bananas — and they weren't exactly wrong.

"I'll ask," *next time,* I didn't add.

Haunting of Echoes

"I DON'T LIKE IT," Maya pouted in the lobby of the redone flatiron.

I didn't either, but kept it to myself since people were around. I didn't feel particularly up to fielding the crazy stares engendered by talking to the ghost of a building right then.

"Totally trashed the place," she sneered at the posh bullshit inflicted on history. Molly would have been furious — Maya... more complicated. The building had been her haunt for I don't know how long, up until recent developments. She made rude gestures and childish faces at the bellhops scurrying about and the tourists plushing themselves on velvet chairs.

The immaturity was humorously incongruous to Maya's currently mature form — red full lips, swinging curves, and curly short hair framing the face of a queen. I had the strangest feeling it may be the closest face to hers she'd yet worn, though I don't know what led me to believe that.

Hope maybe? Hope that she was coming into sync with her true self and that maybe she could get herself outta the mess she was in? She hadn't pulled out the bagpipes in ages that I was aware of — or the screaming red dress — but then there hadn't been much opportunity to.

Rewind a bit before Last Christmas — WHAM — when Maya got evicted.

"Missed your sparkles." I picked some tinsel out of her hair and gave Maya a kiss. She'd set off a glitter bomb in the midst of the construction workers gutting the flatiron — no one noticed, though a few of their wives had questions later that eve. Not only is it the STD of crafting, it's the mark of titty bars everywhere.

"They can't *do* this to me!" Dismay filled her voice.

It was sad. The whole werewolf cop movie put the building on certain people's radar — especially the haunting stories from behind the scenes, which went viral. The clip of Naked-Maya or no-Naked-Maya ran 'round the internet as fast as that striped dress — people loved to argue on the internet. Off, too.

And it did bring attention, which was exactly what Maya had wanted — just the wrong kind. The kind that whispers greed into fetid ears and rots the edifices of legacy. Not the kind that would relieve her perdition.

I'd wanted to help her, but as I stood amongst the ruination being wrought, I'd been too late. Best I could do at the time was loose the tether binding her to the place and send her Molly's way. Happy Merry.

How the world goes and changes on you when you aren't looking. Lose focus for a second, and it happens. The flatiron I knew vanished in a blink of scaffolding and flapping tarp while I'd looked away.

Maya snuggled up beside, lacing her arm through mine as she fit her curves pleasantly against me, pulling me out of the building and into the crisp mountain air.

"I can't stand to look at it," she buried her face in my shoulder to keep from seeing. Change was hard. At least outside it still looked the same — save for the hotel marquee and valet stand. They'd cleaned away the decades of soot and smog from the stone, leaving it a pinkish-grey hue where once it looked like so much smudge.

Down the street we went to get somewhere warm, winding up at the Times where I ordered mochas for the both of us — they'd ignored Maya per ushe. No doubt they wondered why I'd ordered two.

"I think I remember a bit more now," she said, twirling her curls as we waited for the drinks. "I found this newspaper clip when they bashed down a basement wall I didn't know was there."

Or she accidentally-maybe-on-purpose forgot?

"And it was talking about this protest that got rowdy," she circled around the topic. I wondered what the protest was for, wondered just how long Maya had been lost. Civil rights? Vietnam? AIDS epidemic? Prohibition? "There was this face," she pointed to the one she wore, "and it just kinda felt right."

She flashed it a moment, casting it in flux to an exact replica of the photo — pearls around her neck and on her ears; curls a bit longer, peeking out from under a felt Cloche hat — I like my hats, okay?; and dark, dramatic makeup from the golden age of Hollywood. She looked like a movie star.

Might *have* been — Maya certainly had a flair for the dramatic and penchant for theatrics.

"Oh why thank you ever so much, my lovely," case in point, "Carl," she read the name tag of the barista, who fully ignored her. "You're ever so kind to me. A credit to your profession," she laid it on thick while Carl, with the handy-dandy name tag, slid both mochas my way.

"Double-fisting sorta day?" Do better, Carl. "Sure is cold out, huh?"

"Thanks a latte," I returned volley, not that he'd waited to see how badly his joke landed. At least the coffees were hot.

Maya groaned at my pun as I slid her drink over — not that she got to enjoy it.

"You need better material," Olya —
I-told-you-she-wasn't-Helena — scoffed and sat in the
empty chair next to me, opposite Maya, pulling the latte
in front of her. "Know I taught you better than that," she
sipped.

"Hey! That's mine, you two-bit street hussy," Maya fumed.
"No! Two-bit's waaaaay too much for your *services*," she
scathed, though Olya paid no mind.

"You're being incredibly rude," I glared. Maya stopped short
of launching her next tirade, used to saying whatever the hell
she wanted to anyone, anywhere, because it didn't matter
half a damn. "Both of you," I included Olya.

Con-woman through and through, and totally lacking
impulse control, she'd swiped the latte without a second
thought. Didn't matter that it was Maya's — Olya saw her —
she wanted the mocha latte and took it while Maya simply
let her, reacting only after the fact.

"You can see me?" Maya got a little hesitant. She'd been seen
a lot of late — thanks to the Last Chance and, frankly, being
in my orbit of *other* — and lost the jubilant outbursts she'd
once had, thinking herself finally free.

"You're there, aren't ya?" Olya took another sip. Gentleman
softy that I am, I slid Maya mine.

"What do you want?" We hadn't parted on great terms, Olya
and I, but that's the game sometimes. "I'm not exactly happy
to see you."

"Master," she lowered her eyes, "if I'd known it was you." She
looked young — younger than I'd seen her since I gave her
the key. Odd.

"Save it," I grumbled. "Me or not, you sold out a student of
the school. You treat all the pupils like that?"

"If the need fits," she demurred. "Besides, pupils worthy of
the school aren't so easily bested, are they, sir?" She had a
point — the Saffron School didn't turn out weaklings.

"She calls you sir, too, huh?" Maya flashed to her leathers —
every inch a wicked queen. "Maybe we can play," she flexed
her riding crop.

"Delightful," the silver-haired pixie-girl flashed overly large
eyes Maya's way at the invitation. Hoo-boy, this could get
raunchy quick — both upping their ante.

"Enough." I could feel the headache forming. "Again I ask,
what do you want, Olya? Don't make me ask a third."

"There's a problem at the school," pretense fell from her
face. She wasn't trying to run a con anymore.

"Guessed that much thanks to your stunt."

"Yes, well," she swallowed. "You weren't around, so I did
what you told me to do: look after the school," she allowed
herself a moment of pride. "Worked, too! Got payment from
that stingy devil up front," she laughed. "This happened
after, though."

"So, the problem?"

"Kinda broke the clock." Olya-no-longer-named-Helena
held her hands out, palms up, showing off a bit of
re-acquired youth.

Hoo-boy.

"If you hear your name," I started our trek in the woods with
the warning, "no, you didn't." It'd suck if one of the ladies got
spirited away by the local lurkers and displaced deities —
they'd gotten a little pushy once faith came in short supply.
But the bones of the world remembered.

"My name is whatever you call me," Evette blinked at me,
stepping on a twig. She was slightly out of her element, sans

Last Chance, but Hank had sent her along on this girls-only trip.

"Get back to the kiss." Deirdre had missed out on that bit while Zestra was at the wheel. Seemed her love for tea extended beyond the loose-leaf variety.

"Aren't you a seer?" I countered. "Can't you just take a peek?" I was still majorly conflicted about the whole fiasco. "In fact, please do!" Maybe she could tell me if it'd been Felix or Asher behind the wheel when the lips locked.

"I can't while I'm walking," she pouted. Deirdre was down for a girls' trip, too, and totally wasn't coming along as our Uber. Walking wherever she liked did save us a bit on the trip though.

"No chewing gum either?" *That* she giggled at in her ever-effervescent way. She popped a bubble. Show off.

"*That*, I can do. Seeing is different," she smacked her gum again. "Dish?"

"I'd need a few more drinks," I deflected. I had the offering, but it was best not to offend winter incarnate by stealing a nip.

"Fresh out, mistress," Evette shrugged after habitually reaching for a pour. How long had it been since she'd gotten out?

"Molly," I corrected out of habit. "You're off the clock, Evette." Technically, anyway. She was the muscle for this trip, according to Hank, which I thought was entirely unnecessary. He'd gotten way overprotective when he heard I was going to meet death.

"No, nuh uh, no way," he'd crossed his arms. "I'm coming with."

"Nope, she doesn't like men." I patted his arm and gave him a conciliatory kiss. "Sweet as you are. No boys allowed."

"Take Evette, then," the old devil hrmphed, concerns mildly assuaged. "Dependable."

Which was totally okay with me — she was no Garth, but show me a bartender who can't handle her own and I'll know she's not a bartender. Besides, we'd never had a girls' night out.

Back to the woods was the last place I'd thought I'd be going, but here's the thing. I had Hank's favor in my pocket, so that'd get Felix-Asher to do it, but I still needed the how, and I'd just run into the perfect person to ask about that out in the wylde.

Snow blanketed the woods, giving it an odd hush only broken by Evette's careless feet occasionally snapping a twig or finding a bare leaf patch. Deirdre's feet were lithe, and the effect of her walking caused everything around us to blur and shift in slightly nauseating fashion — I tried to keep my eyes on the women walking with me.

"I haven't gotten to ask," I turned to the reader. "Are you recovering well after," I paused, "you know." I couldn't quite bring myself to say 'pulling your soul apart like taffy' as I'd so blithely put it to Felix.

"Oh totally," she beamed. "Best thing that could have happened. My hospital TikToks went super viral, and I was able to help sooo many people." Ever the silver lining with Deirdre. "I've been volunteering there since I got out. They were so kind to me."

"Something's watching us," Evette broke in.

"We're in the middle of the woods," I replied. "Of course something's watching. You're never alone in the woods. The question is whether the one we want to talk to gets the message."

"Hello the woods," Deirdre chimed, all cheerful. "We're totally not suspicious folk and just want to talk to a friendly spirit of death if one's around. If she's not, we're just gonna chill for a bit if you want to join in. No judgments!"

Well, that oughta work. I stared dumbfounded at her audacity. I guess you never know unless you ask.

A chill blew through my bones as the moonlight dimmed. I'd not felt her touch since the coldest nights of my youth. Nights so cold running sap froze, exploding trunks of the unwary and old. Hush fell upon us as Calley — Felix and his idiotic names — landed among us.

"Lady Thousand-Winters," I bowed my head. Deirdre and Evette followed suit.

"Yes yes, be not scared, my child." She lifted a hand under her robe to wave off the formalities. "Come pay tribute in my shrine. It's fucking cold," she pulled her thick white robe closed. "You brought the wine, right?"

Rent paid or not, there wasn't much time left for the Saffron School — according to the broken clock embedded in the sidewalk at the corner of Shaw Street and Place. Polished bronze casing the size of a manhole cover flush with the granite surround, the hands read quarter of three.

No clue what calamitous mishap had caused the enormous crack in the crystal face — the damn thing had survived a century of horses and cars, errant jackhammers and dozers, and the occasional bomb blast — but there it sat, losing time.

Leaking, more like — and it stank.

Everyone thinks time must smell like old books or ancient libraries — dust, biblichor, a hint of mildew, and, surprisingly, lime. Maybe even an unearthed tomb — a gust of stale death mingled with fresh air once the seal breaks, complete with curses. But no, it's much more synthetic than that — being mostly a human concept.

Time has an actinic tinge to its scent from metallic pieces grinding against one another with somewhat warmer pottery notes mixed in — that fired earth smell ceramics have with the texture of jangled nerves as one runs their hand over the parched clay.

"What'd you do?" I didn't really think she could have done anything — even on accident. That sort of thing doesn't happen, but that'd been happening far too frequently for my liking of late.

"Nothing!" Her protest earnest. "Heard this giant CRACK one day during class — so loud I felt it rip through my heart," Olya grabbed her chest, "and found it like this."

No doubt it hit hard. The clock kept the Saffron School pinned in place — like the lantern's flame the Last Chance. But instead of time spent here being uncounted against the seconds of one's life, it seemed to pause the world around. It allowed students endless hours of practice to refine their tricks and trade as society waited with bated breath. But now that chronological bubble had burst, forcing them back into the eddies and currents sweeping us all along.

"And since I just found you again after all these years," she played coy. "I thought maybe you could fix it. Seemed stronger than a coincidence — as things tend to be with you, sir." Flattery and guilting at my absence — I'd taught her well.

"Only one person I know can fix *that*," I nodded at the leaking clock. Same prodigal artificer who fixed mine. Guilt stabbed me once more as I missed him — so many things I'd taken for granted and more left unsaid.

"Great!" Olya delighted in counterpoint, hopping with a clap of her hands. "Let's go get him! You've got my..." she paused, correcting herself, "er, your key, yes?"

"Can't," I sighed. "He died."

"Guess that settles that," Maya added unhelpfully. "Nothing to be done about your stinky clock," she crinkled her nose. "But seeing as he was in the middle of fixing *my* problem..."

"Toots," Olya took one long look, "your problem is easy. Same as it was when you left the school eighty-some-odd years ago, Miss Maya Isabel Rubido."

"I've never..." Maya began, but I knew the denial rang untrue — too much fit.

"You, dearie," Olya smushed and stretched Maya's face. "Deep deep down, you cower and cringe and desire desperately *not* to be seen."

Before Maya could rebut, a susurrus of cricket wings rose, rushing along the sidewalk outside number One-Twenty Shaw Street in Pembreton Oaks — a place forgotten by time, but not the creatures that ate it.

"Chronovores." My heart dropped, eyes darting between the leaking clock and the winding doors of the Saffron School — stench of time drawing the vores like locusts.

"And that's the second problem," Olya hightailed it inside. I grabbed Maya and hustled after, reluctantly following suit as the plague coated everything in dark.

"Should totally dump that jerk," Calley sipped her wine. "He's no good for you. Not to mention he's totally obsessed with his ex."

Aww, said ex echoed in my head. *He's always been a sweetie.* I giggled.

Deirdre giggled, too. *Hushup, you,* I thought at her as I sipped more wine. Maybe I'd had a little much.

"It's not like that with us," I blushed.

"But it could be," Deirdre, again, way too privy to each of us. "I've seen things," she nodded resolutely. "You've been important to him for a while now."

"I'm with the death goddess," Evette weighed in — wine at least got rid of the whole 'mistress' deference. "You can do better."

"Come, come," Deirdre slipped to the backseat, letting Zestra at the wheel. "He is a worthy lover," she smiled. "This I know... eeewwww," Deirdre popped back mid-thought. "TMI Grandma," she shuddered.

We all burst out laughing.

"Matron and Maid as one," Calley approved. "The old ways live," she toasted.

"The old ways," I raised my glass. "Does that make me the crone, then?" I was pretty young for a Trenynn, but I did have some years on Deirdre *and* her grandmother.

Calley cleared her throat. "I do believe that honor belongs to dear Evette," she tipped her glass toward my bartender who sipped her wine most dignified.

I'll be honest, I didn't know much about Evette aside from her bartenderiness and stout regard for the rules. Sure, I never tried all that hard, but she didn't volunteer much, either. Mental note: *Get Evette drunk more often.*

"You don't look a day over thirty," I baited.

"By design," she let slip. "Young enough to get good tips, old enough not to be constantly hit on. It's my preferred appearance, though, should you wish me to change..." An eyebrow rose.

"As long as you're comfortable," I shrugged. "But come on," I had to know, "how old?"

"At last count, seven hundred and forty-three," she didn't even blink. "Human years," she clarified. "That's how long since I was summoned. Before that..." Evette shrugged.

"Your skin is flawless." Deirdre got a little too close for Evette's comfort. "What's your routine?"

Calley and I giggled as the young reader tried her damnedest to find a pore on the demon's face while suggesting she start a YouTube channel for beauty advice — she could be the next big thing!

"So," I sighed, getting to the reason I was here. "If I could make it stick," I laid out the need for a failsafe should Asher break free, "how does it work?"

"First," winter incarnate turned her moon-saucer eyes toward me, "being dead and not being alive are two different things." The death spirit drained her wine glass and began explaining death and its many applications in the world writ large. Of particular interest were the gates through which the living could pass beyond.

"I see plan fingers," Calley refilled her wine, conspiracy of a smile on her face.

It was all coming together, much as it sickened me.

I hated it — never wanted to use it. But what you want to do, what you can do, and what you have to do are tragically different.

"Well, I'll be damned," I stated the obvious. Not really new information, just something you say. "I forgot what hellishness awaited beyond these doors."

Karaoke faced off with full orchestras. Mimes pantoed the words ventriloquists put in their mouths — an absurd improv. All while pick- and put- pockets circulated tracer bills among gathered gawkers playing pretend.

The bombshell Olya'd dropped of my shady sometimes lover still rippled shockwaves, but on we pressed — returning to the scene of her unhinge, perhaps to jog the traumas loose.

"It's really not so bad," Maya fit right in the cacophony, breaking off to mingle in the noise — running to and fro. Olya simply stepped out of sight.

Klaxons sounded as the scene flooded with red lights — someone failed a lift.

"Out-fucking-standing." The slow-clap that followed the sarcastic praise froze everyone in place on the training floor. "Who wants to tell me what numbnuts did wrong?"

Lankily tall, he leaned lazily — holding up the wall, one might say — nondescript as any doof on the street, save for the bad mustache crawling across his face. That was new. So was his overseeing the training floor — one of his skill ought to be out merrily mayheming. Maybe it was the latest in a series of terrible life choices.

"Jo-Jo there," I didn't know his name, "flubbed the handoff to Roy-Boy," his either, "while Leslie," nope, "and Abby's flim-flam gambit is mildly embarrassing. That about cover it, Ricky?" His name I knew.

"You forgot the guy playing Galaga in the corner," the trainer in charge of the floor snarked.

"Everyone noticed him," I rolled my eyes. "Should've picked up on the rest, too," I clasped hands with my fellow con. Asshole lifted my watch.

"Losing your touch, Felix," Ricky snickered, holding my bait watch up as his pants fell around his feet.

"And you're losing more than that," I snapped his belt. "Nice boxers." Plaid, classic.

Ricky's face turned red and he snatched his belt back, shuffling closer to wrap me in a big hug. "Asshole."

"Put your pants back on," I patted his back. "The hell you doing training new recruits? Where's Norvin?"

Not-Helena wasn't the only instructor at the Saffron School for Confidence — not when I'd founded it. Not when I attended it, either. In fact, she wasn't the one teaching most of the students — bad match, that. Not many can process her... eccentricities.

Norvin, though, was fantastic with the freshies — skill surpassed only by his patience. Really helped get my feet under me again after my dip. Turned Ricky right around, too.

"Not here," Ricky's face went dark. Concern. "Helena didn't tell you?"

I refrained from correcting him — here, she *was* Helena. And during uncertainty she needed to *stay* Helena.

"Alright kiddos," Ricky clapped his hands once — not that he needed to get their attention. I don't think any had looked away after our less than private tête-à-tête. "Switch it up!"

That was the cue to swap places. All the mimes and orchestral distractions would take the role of thieves while those who'd been plying nimble fingers would now act a fool. Good to practice all the roles we must play — gets rid of the shy and the nerves. Really commit to the bits, too. Much easier to get a decade of stagecraft at the Saffron School than even the off-off-off-Broadwayiest show — all to believe the bit.

Really quite remarkable to see the change from without — full strike of all the scenery, bring in the new, throw in some chairs for the ad hoc theater. I was trying to figure out just what play was afoot when I saw Maya among the Weird Sisters, looking all ragged and filthy in her trappings, carrying cliched staves as two others wheeled out the cauldron to bubble.

"Macbeth," slipped off my tongue before I could catch it. Fuck. I needed to be more careful or Asher'd rattle the cage once more. "Be right back." I made to leave the school and make the requisite leftward laps and thrice spit.

Ricky stopped me cold, face graven. "Best to not, at least right now," he shook his head. "That's what got Norvin. Things have been all kinds of wonky lately."

Wonky, good word for it.

Chill settled deeper to my bones as fates further sealed, unable to assuage the geas of the Scottish Play.

"By the pricking of my thumb," the lady of death intoned as Deirdre and I stood to either side of the onyx gate covered in black bramble — Evette would not venture near the oculus to the afterworld.

Beyond the bramble curled and coiled in upon itself, a deep fog beckoned me to cross, whispering tendrils toward me as I stood too close, watching Lady Thousand-Winters in the ceremony I'd conduct should the need arise.

Delicately, she gifted a single drop of blood to the thirsty vines — the red life drinking away as the thorny veil parted. I felt it then — *l'appel du vide*, the French call it.

Call of the void.

I couldn't see what lay behind the mists released from their binds, writhing and beckoning. Reaching out to caress my skin. To taste me.

"I hear them laughing," Deirdre said, tears near to her eyes. "There's pure joy, and..." She took a step. "NO CHILD." Her voice was that of Zestra in an instant.

I'd never felt the gypsy soul so present in the medium before, but it only made sense as my eyes traveled back to the portal — she was just *over there*. One step beyond the cold.

"It's a one-way trip." A hand landed on my shoulder. I didn't realize I'd moved. Deirdre and I stood shoulder to shoulder, one step from beyond when Thousand-Winters brought our sense back about us.

One, the Rembrancer's voice echoed.

Clocksucker

"IT'S NOT LIKE I *want* something cataclysmic to happen," Molly defended.

"So, in order to accomplish this non-cataclysmic happening," I drew out my scathe, adding more words from which it could drip, "you find my nemesis and the thorn that's dug straight into my side each lifetime," pause for effect, "the creature who doxxed this face and form so that compounding bounties might be collected," glare here, "and bring him RIGHT TO ME?" I couldn't believe it. "On purpose?" It hurt.

"It be so. It be so," the vermin spilled verbose. "It be Bill o'deSoul," with a split of his rotting teeth — one seemed to be now missing. I shot Molly a side-eyed brow. "Pox, plague, and blight be," the Bloodybell started up his cursing — pointy fingers aimed my way.

"Flip it, reversed, and reflected at thee," I flashed an Uno card for shiggles. The fucker didn't deserve to be taken seriously, yet visceral violence urged deep inside.

"Aye, 'tis the words of rot you cast upon my blameless self," the goblin glared, stripping his shirt half-off, showing purple-green putrefaction. "Thus a kindness if you please," hand out held pro forma, he grimaced.

"Fine," I gritted my teeth. "Let's get this over with," I gestured to the little paddle boat bobbing in the lake. Damn thing was shaped like a duck. "After you, Bloodybell." Never turn your back on them.

"Have you the aqua vitae?" He meant scotch. I always have that.

"Don't leave home without it." I flashed the label of a bottle pulled from the twist — a Jura I'd been saving. Fitting to put quits to this nuisance over. "Cheese, too." Cheese was cheese — I felt Molly's disapproval without seeing the glare she no doubt gave.

Bill nodded satisfaction and hopped in the duck, lightly wobbling over little waves.

"Where's my seat?" Molly toed the tail of the rubber boat, testing its buoyancy.

"Over there," I pointed to a bench on the lakeshore.

"No, you're not ditching me," hand on hip. As much as I'd longed for her presence of late. To know I hadn't driven her away for good. To fall back into the familiar comforts of our friendship. Right now, she'd only confuse matters.

"I'm not ditching you," I promised, hopping in the novelty. No lie, despite how it looked. "We're just going to have a little heart-to-heart and sort this out," I smiled.

"Touching hearts," Bill also smiled, "is what I desire as well." He skissed his sharpened claws and laughed like shredding metal.

"Don't kill him," Molly frowned.

"I'll do my best." Lighthearted fakery in full effect. No guarantees.

"As will I," the murder-hobo didn't help. No doubt he meant *to* kill me.

"Save it for the island," I glared, peddling the duck out solo — goat-man's legs working backward and all. Besides, he seemed distinctly *less* of late.

Molly'd said he'd acquitted himself well on their journey — gleefully gacking bumpers front left and center, but he'd also been bested and bruised by some the Bloodybell never need've feared. Veritable terror, they were and given wide berth for much more than their odious countenance.

And then there was the bounty — outsourcing deeds done dirty was entirely out of character for the stabbing enthusiast. Even if he was getting up there in centuries.

"Don't fret, dear foe," I borrowed a line from Ez B. "I won't send you for a dunk, much as it may improve the stench," I assured the creature angrily staring at the water. "You've my word."

"The word of a charlatan," Bill ground. "Worth not even the air spent to utter."

This was going to be such a fun trip, I sighed. What was Molly thinking?

"Be safe," I whispered after he was out of earshot. *Asshole,* I didn't add aloud.

I'd been thinking how badly Felix'd been reacting to the surprise attacks. Hector and Helena's betrayal, Gregory's ambush, Fulcanelli's fuckery, and all the nameless bumpers slaughtered without so much as a 'how do you do?'

They needed to stop before... well before I lost him. Either to himself or rando assailant number three. So after visiting with Thousand-Winters and giving myself massive anxiety over *that* particular plan, I decided it might be a brilliant idea to stop the bear-poking attacks at the source — Bill o'deSoul.

Decided we should make a little pit-stop on our way back from the afterworld.

Finding him had been remarkably easy — I, well *we*, cheated. Not like Felix does or anything, but a little esoteric aid from Deirdre's spirit guides teamed up with a little Google-Fu and tracked the rat bastard to a corrugated self-storage middle of BFE *somewhere*.

That got me close enough, at least — I made Deirdre and Evette wait outside.

BANG BANG BANG on the roll-up door, reverb rattling in a ripple up and down its tracks. Always knock thrice.

"I know you're in there, Bill o'deSoul!" My nose had led the rest of the way. I'd gotten used to his archaic tongue, but the halitosis that came with it... never.

"Be I though? Be any who so languish upon the world truly *there*?" It sounded like the murder-hobo drew a lonesome claw across the metal — making a SKRISS.

"Are you drunk?" I'd never seen the murder-hobo partake, even when we were besieged at the bar — many of us were drinking our way through that.

"Oh ho no, not yet! For that, I'm biding my time to be with the charlatan on the island." Ah, Whisky Island — more properly, the Isle of Conversation. Felix had claimed it a time-honored Scottish tradition — get drunk on a deserted island and sort your shit out. Quite reasonable, really.

"Wanna open the door so we can talk?" I kicked the roll-up, much to Bill's cursing — apparently he'd been leaning against it.

"Pox and plague," he cursed. "Unless you've come with his heart on a platter," he spat, "your words hold no interest of mine." He seemed... sulky?

"And if I said I am his heart, in part," here was the gamble, "and can get your meeting moved up?" I slipped a smooth stone into my hand — one of two gifts given to me by a spirit of death.

Bold, the echo in my soul approved.

The door rumbled up just enough for a yellowed goat eye to peer out, the rest hidden in shadow. "And if I kill you now, heart-in-part, what glorious anguish he'd suffer. So generous of you," he hacked.

"If you kill me now…" I countered, a bit glib. My hand felt for the hole worn through the stone, readying to see. "…you'll never get your meet-cute," I furthered my gamble, jerking the door up higher to get a good look at the murder-hobo through the hag's eye — a smooth river stone with a hole worn through.

Bill cringed as the light spilled in and an intense wave of odor, out. And not his usual stench — vile sickness. Fester and foulness aerosolized, nearly weaponized — if he had the energy for malice.

"Or your fix." He'd been talking a good game as always, but the putrid husk given to delirium spoke otherwise. Further confirmed by the hag's eye — which revealed hidden depths. Whatever curse Felix had put to him was taking its toll — fetid miasma oozed from the goblin. Death stalked near.

"This rot I'll always live with," his face cracked a bone-tooth smile. "This rot that will be the death of me. But for every silver second he squanders," he flashed a coin — a coin much like the one Felix gave him to go away in the corn maze, "a renewed me I be to take the vengeance I seek."

The murder-hobo stuck the coin in his mouth, biting with broken teeth to nip a bit of the silver away. Scarred and misshapen, the coin showed each glaring bite — he'd been saving this one. As he suckled the silver second, vigor returned to his wilted form — seemingly reversing the creeping decay.

"Will that one, slim silver last until the appointed whisky day? No?" I didn't let him answer. "I didn't think so. Then hear me out…"

"It's no Eilean a' Chombraidh," I landed the duck on our own private whisky island, "but it'll do for our chat."

Sure, the actual island had a certain power about it — years of layered ritual do that to a place, plus, c'mon, Scotland — but it was the intent that mattered.

And I intended to settle things between us that had been niggling at me for three hundred years or more. Manifest resolution.

"Oh a lovely little chat indeed," the murder-hobo started — noxious breath infiltrating my nostrils. Gleary goat eyes and yellow cracked teeth grinned malevolent.

"Seeing you again, Bill, brings back all these old feelings." I punched him — sucker style straight in the loud mouth.

Fuckface sputtered and spat. "That's for your little stunt at Sassy's," I wiped my hand clean. "We'll figure out how many others after we have this," I slammed the scotch bottle into his gut.

"Unkind and uncouth," Bill held his face, working his jaw. "Ever must I suffer the ignommities," he spat a tooth. Didn't think I'd hit him that hard.

"Why do I hate you so much?" It actually troubled me — every time, it was true — my immediate reaction was one of revulsion. Instinctive brain screamed fear, for obvious reasons, but bubbled memories contained only derision and dismission. "Use those knife fingers and cut the foil on that," I pointed to the bottle in his clutch as I pulled glasses from ethereal nothing. "And why do you hound me so?" Returning to the original thoughtline.

"Make no mistakes, ye hate me not," the Bloodybell grumbled — his signature cape now a dried dull brown.

Caked and crumbly. "Though you I mightily despise," he popped the cork to pour.

"I'll make no mistake if you make some bloody sense," I held out my glass for a civil dram — oddly familiar. "I know it's not because of the curse thing — you were annoying the shit out of me before then. In fact," I threw back the pour, "I only did that because you caught me on my worst day." Breach of etiquette and good scotch to chase the dark thought.

"That did double my detestation. It did," he poured me another. I'd need all the help I could get through this. "T'was but the thousand and first discourtesy done me by you, and that you remember none other adds to my rancor." Bill shot his first dram at that, wincing as the alcohol burned the newly emptied tooth socket.

"Okay." I paused to think over the scotch, trying to properly appreciate it, though I held my breath to keep out the goblin's stench — hard to pick out the spiced fruit notes over egg-rot. "So you're mad I don't remember," I hazarded a guess. "Look, it's been a bit spotty lately..."

"Ye've a clock, I've seen." He'd spied me through my own eyes, in fact. "Surely you've done checked, even if ye did forget."

"Hasn't meant that much to me," I was honest. Maybe a little tipsy — hypoxia is a bitch. "How'd you see me?" I'd been more than curious about that.

"Yer not the only who've tasted of time, charlatan," he pulled a silver second, slipping it into his mouth as he sipped. "Ahhh." Bill allowed a brief moment of enjoyment at the pairing.

As such, I'll allow myself a mild tangent. Time stinks — I've told you that already. But I often find myself contemplating how delicious scotch — the whisky the most steeped in time — is, despite its extreme proximity. And now I wondered just what that particular pairing opened up on the pallet.

"That right there," Bill shoved the glass in my face before I could ask for tasting notes. "That right there," he hopped, mad, "is what vexes and festers so. You ruin me life with a caustic plumb n'to you, it matters not one whit!"

I felt it would only fan the rage if I asked what he was on about at this point, so I let him spit.

"Allow me lay the scene," he triggered a memory of mine. "We wagered a bet on unicorn's breath..."

Back before crackberries or the internet. Guinness wasn't even around yet — the brewery, not the record book they put together — bar bets could get brutal. And this one'd gone horribly wrong.

Seriously, fuck unicorns and the horse they rode in on. They ruin everything. That bet, this chat.

"Speaking calls," I groused as what some might consider a majestic beast grazed its way to our little chinwag — eyes bleeding red, sharp horn stabbing through its head.

"Pox and plague," Bill managed before the beast charged.

"You set me up," I dove to the side. I'd already been flambéd by a horse and lived to tell the tale — rather not get stabbed by one, too. "You rat-faced..."

"'Tis not one of mine," he hissed and skissed, bracing to strike the coming pass. "You see how it attacks me? I *keep* my given word — the bounty be no more."

Head lowered, the parasite pony charged the murder-hobo — gleeful grin on his face. Fucker loved to fight. Springing higher than the stabbing horn, the Bloodybell twisted mid-air, slashing at the flesh rendered impervious to pain.

Wished I had that ribbon bound in Berlyn's bow about now. Fuck. Later.

Now it was my turn to dodge as Bill seemed to gloat. "Thought the beasts dead, you said," a slight smirk twisting his lips.

"Me too," I paused, '*I* said'?

"Ye killed the last," he went on, "ken ye kill the next?"

I'd had the charms then — bubble of a memory. Rather, another me'd had the charms — one given to carnage. Maybe it'd fall for a bucket of sand like the mares?

Not bloody likely, my inner monologue rose, rattling the cage's bars. *Let me free to do the deed. I'll be quick.*

Asher'd been getting louder in my head lately — since my luck began eroding. Slowly, patiently, I worried he'd work himself free — like before.

Shame your tasty tree's not here, I felt him grin. *I hear they like virgins.*

I ignored that, and instead, words I never thought would be uttered were — "Bill," I dodged another pass, "you ever had sex?" Ick. Ack. Hrrrng, the idea made me nauseous.

"What business be it thine?" I really didn't want to think about goblin-sex.

"Apparently they like virgins."

He sprang to the unicorn's back. How'd it even work with legs bent back like that?

"And so naturally, you consider me unworthy of love? Of knowing a woman's delicate touch? Many a lass has enjoyed the attentions of ol' Bill's honeyed-silver tongue," he licked his lips. *Did they grab his horns or...*

Vomit. Right in my mouth. I almost stepped in front of the charging unicorn right then, just to scrub the image from my brain.

Maybe I could burn the thoughts out... duh!

"Where's the scotch?" I sought the bottle not to forget, but because I remembered.

Elliot wasn't the only one who could breathe fire. Pyro 101 was one of the more popular classes at the Saffron School, and I'd loved every second of it. Shame to use such good scotch for a side-show, but needs must. I found the bottle rolled off to the side — stopper still in place, thankfully.

"Lure it over here!" I yanked the stopper with my teeth, one wrist flicking to life my naphtha strike — memento of St Germain — as I readied a mouthful to blow.

Bill bandied about with the beast — knife-like fingers striking and parrying horn thrusts. Every wound he'd tried to give the creature merely a nuisance to the dead horse.

Closer. The fumes burned my sinuses.

Closer. My eyes began to water.

Get out of the way, I don't know why I cared when the goblin came into range. The same part of me that always gifted the silver seconds didn't want him to burn — pity? Or guilt?

I saw it, the bulbous bump at the base of the horn, right where it erupted from the skull — that was my target, its weak spot. Throbbing. Ew.

BURN I sprayed the booze through the indigo flame, tight as I could so it found its target.

And missed.

Well, not entirely. I'd hit the mark, but the mark fled — bursting like a tick, it sprayed me with its blood — the hardened horn dropped off. The host body, though, beat a hasty retreat through the brush. Fuckers burrowed deep like that — fungi that fruited spears instead of 'shrooms.

Bill o'deSoul rose from where he'd crouched, coughing out the smoke. I'd tried not to hit him, honest. But his eyebrows certainly look singed.

"Damn," I spat, "lost a bet." Unicorns did still exist.

For some reason, the Bloodybell found it immensely hilarious — the laughter softening his countenance, the flames seemingly purging his stench.

"Make that two," I realized a bit late.

Hoisted on my own petard.

"What's taking so long?"

I kept checking my phone, it'd been more than four hours. I'd seen Felix kill a bottle of scotch in a third that time. Granted, Sassy had been involved, but Felix drank the whole bottle. Sassy'd had his own cask. Had no clue what kind of drunk the murder-hobo was.

"Maybe Bill's a sloshed sweetheart?" *Nah.*

I stared out at the island through the hag stone, seeing if the pall of death fell over it. Calley had shown me that trick for later — in case I needed to use the favor and force Felix through the gate, I'd need to be able to see it. Personally, I hoped the other gift tucked safely away in a flask worked first.

That would come later, though. After the island.

All I'd seen through the eye was a green flash, then gone. Not sure what that was, but they hadn't killed each other.

"Yet," I muttered.

It was a distinct possibility.

I looked back at my phone and through the hag stone once more.

"That's strange," I thought aloud, seeing a familiar red line form at my feet running off to... "You've got some nerve! I oughta..."

Didn't even get to slap the rat bastard before it all went black.

"Your future self left little breadcrumbs," Bill got cryptic on the return trip. Even a little smug. I'd given him a few more kindnesses to go with the remainder of the scotch, and to assuage my guilty conscience. Still owed him a tower.

Guy named Ben once told me: "Whatever is begun in anger, ends in shame." I'd told him to go fly a kite — this was back in my Asher days — think he went on to invent electricity or some shit. Go figure.

But I digress. The aphorism held true.

It'd all started as a mistake, embarrassing as it was. A mistake between... well, not friends. Bill and I'd never been that, no. Just random strangers encountered on the other's particularly bad days left to fester.

Turns out he wasn't a bad sort after all — handy in a fight if he wasn't trying to skewer you. Not that he'd ever succeeded with me — luckily. Didn't want to press it these days, though, so I actually heard the asshole... grr... habits. I actually heard him out sans all my preconceived faults.

"Clocksucker," I called him as he bit a silver second clean in two. I still didn't like him, but the hate assuaged with a bit of the guilt, so it was the best insult I could muster.

He laughed. Exaggeratedly om-nom-nom-nomming his stash. Couldn't help a giggle at the antics.

The miracles of Eilean a' Chombraidh. Friends become
faster and enemies garner less enmity — often misplaced to
begin with.

The world does that to people. Fucking sucks, too. I've
flipped off my fair share of terrible drivers — and they
all deserved it — doesn't mean I should'a done it though.
What's the worst that could happen? They flip me back? No.

Never know what sort of cascades shit like that can cause,
what'll cause a person to come epically unhinged.

One second, you're paddling a duck boat across a lake,
the next you're staring at a ransom note where your friend
should be.

A threat.

Neatly typed on a three-by-five.

The Improbable Sword

I'VE NEVER BEEN A father, and chances are, never will
be. But I imagined this was what it's like — in part
— as I stared at the unmoving body of the glorious
and illustrious, unduplicable — and many have tried
— egregiously loquacious, totally bodacious immortal
alchemist the Compte de St Germain.

The hideously consumptive corruption itself had abated
once the Pullet's soul had been plucked, but the scars
remained — the toll taken. Sassy'd said it simply melted
away as he'd stood vigil.

Still, he didn't wake in the flickering lantern light. A
real marvel, that — his handiwork. Simply elegant. Like a
Chinese paper lantern released in memory of the departed, it
floated by his bedside — steadily bobbing up and down as he
no longer breathed, but lingered near. The construction was
clever — delicate wire frame suspended from the luminary,
a simple tray with a wick lit alight, fueled by the dregs of his
elixir.

He'd made it so Molly could freely leave the Last Chance
— back before a piece of my Dena had been grafted to
her Trenynn soul. Seemed only right to replace the poor
imitation I'd made in haste with this original masterpiece
as he lay to rest.

I could do nothing else but worry and fret, like a parent
whose child is sick, keeping watch.

"Nothing makes sense," I told my prone friend. "Not one fucking bit."

I'd been trying to sort it all out and came here to think. Sassy-pants let St Germain keep the room, and every once in a while, he or Elvis would check on him, seeing if there was any change. But both were out and about right then, so we had the place to ourselves.

Wasn't sure what Sassy was off to do — he had a very busy social calendar and loved visiting various old haunts. Elvis, well he just wanted some diner food every now and then and to get out and prove he was still alive — loved all those National Enquirer bits. Side note, that particular publication had no idea Elvis really was hiding out with Bigfoot — just making shit up — they never made any appearances together. But, blind squirrel and all.

He twitched.

There went that train of thought. He did that sometimes — twitch, I mean. Derail my thoughts, too, but that was expected. The twitching was new-ish.

Once, he'd been violently shaking — like he was cold, but forgot how to dance. Up until that point I hadn't been sure, but that proved all soul had left his body — the man could dance, that much was certain. Still, I kept waiting for some sign he'd come back.

Call it a gut feeling.

"Focus." I ran through the problems again. So many, all at once. Wouldn't it be nice if the cataclysms all formed an orderly queue so as to be dealt with in a timely manner and with the care and attention each one deserved?

"They took Molly," I shot StG a meaningful look. *They* being Fulcanelli, formally known as Problem 2 for this incident — the last alchemist was alive. "You really know how to pick 'em." Oh for two on the students.

Problem 1 was obviously the aforementioned missing Molly. I'd seen red and almost immediately launched into a full blown attack seeking a target. And with Molly absent to counsel cool, the Bloodybell of all people was the one to advise, well, not-immediate-mass-murder.

"She be a tough and capable woman, your Molly," he'd said rightly. "She'll be fine so long as you use that cunning luck, she will. Now," he grinned with a skiss, "what fool left this." There was the Bill I knew and despised.

The *this* in question was Problem 3 — the neatly typed three-by-five. It gave me pause.

It was one from the Index, of that I was certain — signed Fulcanelli. That alone gave me lots and lots of questions, but what did he want with St Germain's ring?

"You might know." I wished I could ask — could do a lot of things. Sometimes I worried he'd slip away if I took my eyes off him. Others, it seemed like the alchemist would wake any second.

"When I move, you move," I raised my arm in tune. St Germain didn't.

"Not like that," I sighed, returning to my list of shit. Three major pieces in play and that didn't even begin to cover the grander schemes shifting the pillars of reality.

The Scriptorum, violated — the myriad disasters it caged set loose. The Index, missing — though presumably Fulcanelli had gained some sort of access. Phage-o-vores, feeding rampantly — bad news, whichever dead tongue name you went with. Shambles, everywhere — broken clocks, death spirits loose, rents past due, luck run thin...

"Bad luck to rock an empty chair, dear boy," a voice startled me. They were everywhere in Sassy-pants' ramshackle haven — on the porches, in the yard, out in the woods, and in every room. I'd been absently fidgeting as I thought through the knotted clusterfuck, my toe tipping the rocker back and forth. I turned back to St Germain in the bed, looking for signs of renewed animus — nothing.

"Invites the spirits in," Rakozy's voice came again, this time seated in the chair he now rocked.

"So you're a spirit, now, not a figment?" The face again resembled the one which stared out from his ring on my finger, but he'd discarded the previous frippery — electing instead a simple, silk robe.

"Why must you always be so mule-headed stubborn?" The apparition threw his hands up in disgust.

"The world may never know," I grinned, quoting a scholarly owl.

"I enjoy a good bit of levity myself, dear boy," Rakozy sighed, "but must everything be a joke?"

"The funny stuff." I dug in.

"Was I ever this annoying?" Great. "I know he's me," Asher stepped in from behind, a little to the left. "Part of me, anyway."

"Wrong, buddy," I spun on my shadow. "*I'm* me," I patted my chest, "and you're the crap bits I sacked," I told myself. "I don't need you, not anymore."

"*That's* where you're wrong," Asher straightened at my provocation, cracking his neck. "Why's everything going to shit if you don't need me?"

"Boys, boys," Rakozy clapped. "Focus."

"He started it," Asher grumbled. Petty? Me? "Locking me in a cage with his bullshit." I wanted to punch him.

"Need I remind that *you* built the cage?" A raised eyebrow to quell a storm.

"Rather you didn't," Asher flipped the dead alchemist off. Yep, I wasn't a very nice guy. He flopped on a chair — one that didn't rock — and kicked a boot up on a table. A knife stuck from the top. He was certainly of another era — I could imagine him honing an improbable sword as he sat, ready for violence. "And you," he turned back to me, "where're my manners, eh?? Offer us a beer already."

"Seeing as you're not actually here," I eyed each subconscious projection, "and will be departing soon regardless," I cleared my throat, "I see no need." But I could certainly use one.

"Dear boy, you desperately need some therapy," Rakozy sipped some apparent wine, gracefully swaying. "Siggy might be help! I would very much like to..."

"No thanks," I cut him off. Freud was full of it — not everything was about sex. Carl, on the other hand, had made some astute observations. "What's Fulcanelli want with your ring?" I held up my pinky with his cameo in amber.

"Fulcanelli? Nothing, long dead," Rakozy's face turned bitter for a moment. "The pretender..." he left it hanging. "Well let's see what we can do."

The prince moved off his rocker and stood inspecting the cozy Count of St Germain in the bed, paying particular attention to the lantern floating just above. It was hard to reconcile the image — the same man from two points of his life and death. "I see, I see," he mumbled. "I've entered the egg," he grinned. "How marvelous," gleaming eyes flickered toward me.

Egg?

Rakozy waggled his fingers in the luminary light bathing my friend's body, casting a shadow upon the corpse — the prince grinned and began making signs and symbols.

"What are you..." I moved to interrupt, but my own shadow — the hand of Asher — restrained me. "Let go!" I tried to rip my arm away, finding it pinned by iron. The ring glowed and nearly burned my finger.

"Helping," Rakozy finished his work. A single point above both alchemists' hearts glowed faintly with a beat as the amber dulled. "Now," he turned toward me and my shadow. "Your turn."

"You're one of the lucky ones, you know," Fulcanelli kept talking. Asshole'd been doing that for a while. Definitely one of StG's students, at least in that regard. "Blessed, even! You get to experience every emotion you can possibly feel — all these experiences. Love, heartache, joy, anxiety, euphoria..."

"Being kidnapped, boredom," I rolled my eyes, surreptitiously seeking a way out. Grotesques rudely gestured at me from the carved marble gracefully climbing the domed ceiling above me. As far as prisons went, it was fancy. Pretty, even. Not as pretty as the East Avenue pump station in Baltimore, but what is? Gorgeous, that.

"Not *everyone* gets a soul — even rarer for the Obfirmata such as yourself." I ground my teeth — racist prick. "It pains me to see it wasted so," the asshole pursed his lips.

"*Hylics,* the parrot squawked. "No soul, no soul."

"Et tu, birdbrain?" I spared the parrot a glare — caged as well, though more overtly with gilding and everything. It gleamed in the myriad candle light in the sanctuary beyond.

Nothing shiny for me. In fact, I didn't even realize it *was* a cage until I caught a face full of air when I'd rushed the rat bastard upon coming to. The alchemist had stood smugly in the niche archway — arms crossed, taking a drag from a long-stemmed cigarette holder. Again, judging.

"Should you be smoking in a church?" I'd tired of the lecture and felt like throwing a few jabs. "Or wearing a hat? FYI —

it looks ridiculous." The whole ensemble did — vicar's collar, straight black pants, a flat brimmed Saturno hat straight from seventies SNL, round blackout shades, and were those heels?

"I've always been something of a bad boy," Fulcanelli exhaled a plume of pink smoke my way, only for it to splash off the invisible field holding me in the little alcove off the sanctuary.

"Obviously, Father Sarducci," I shot a dagger at the glam scavenger. Way before my time, but found that comedic rabbit hole one sleepless night.

"How's ya boi?" The parrot flapped in the cage, rather distressed. I was still trying to figure that one out. Felix'd said it was important, or belonged with someone who was. That Fulcanelli had captured it, too, spoke volumes.

"Well last I saw, he was paddling a duck out in the middle of a lake with a murder-hobo set on claiming his heart," I clipped. "So a lot better than me."

"Oh if only that goblin would finish him," the last alchemist sneered. "For your sake and mine. But alas he's proven far more resilient too many times." A sigh and a twinge accompanied the lamentation — an injury? I'd seen a scar above the sneering lip — fresh. What else had gotten ahold of Fulcanelli in the Scriptorum?

"Told you I don't need saving." I was running out of glares and would soon be switching to withering rounds. Maybe even scoffs.

"Have you paid *no* attention to the workings of the wider world?" Bitter rue swelled among the wafting pink smoke as the alchemist gestured with the holder. "We *all* need a little saving with his ilk running amok."

For all the bluster, Fulcanelli was scared of Felix.

Good.

"Every cheat you make shoves us further out of line," my shadow lectured as I fixed my pack. What was I, five?

"It's not *that* bad." Was it?

"Not that b..." Asher found no words. "Do you *know* how many Mandela effects you've caused?" Guess he hit on a stash.

"No idea." Didn't really care either, made good internet sport.

"For one, they named them after the wrong guy," my shadow glared — if it could glare from flat on the pavement.

I don't know exactly what the figment of St Germain had done to link Asher to the shadow I cast, but the result was akin to running the Last Chance — if a bit mouthier. The darker parts of me were still confined, but had a bit more freedom to stretch his legs while not being in control of my body — instead, tethered to. Strangely, it felt as if some pressure had been released.

Took some getting used to — having a sentient shadow again, been a while. Molly'd gotten kinda used to it at the bar, but she was more than happy to leave it with Hank while she frittered about — kinda creeped her out. But, it created options, and *those* I needed right now.

"And they keep spreading." Everyone was a critic. But he had a point — I'd just seen people claiming Ed McMahon never handed out gollywhopping giant checks to people live during the big game. C'mon people, his face was on the envelopes!

Whatever magic the remnant alchemist had worked left him out of the equation — only Asher in the peanut gallery. I figured Rakozy would hitch a ride just to add in his pound of tuppence, but he'd disappeared as soon as we'd left the lantern's light.

"Well how else am I supposed to extricate myself from jams?" That information would come in handy shortly, no doubt, as I found myself inexorably doing something stupid once more.

"Don't get in them to start with," Asher advised, easier said than done. "Be smart about it, old chap. And don't be afraid to get your hands dirty," my shadow turned. "Like me."

"Be like you? I saw what *you* did in the caves," I felt sick again, near to blacking out. "Monster and a maniac, no thank you."

"Yeah, I fucked up," he owned it. "But I'm better now that Dena's safe." Small miracles. "No more coming unhinged. Promise," the shadow crossed its heart.

"Or bloody murder," I'd seen what he'd wrought at the cabin.

"Less blood," my shadow danced ahead. "Got it."

"Less *murder*," I emphasized, adjusting the bag on my shoulder.

"Some people just need killing," Asher rationalized, drawing his blade. Strangely, I felt it in my hand as well, the improbable sword.

"Put that away!" I tried to wipe my hand clean of the weapon's hilt.

The couple waiting for the bus gave me a funny look and shuffled a bit sideways. *Promise I'm not the crazy one*, I thought at them, *my shadow is.*

Saying it aloud wouldn't have helped my case, so I just ducked my head and moved on.

I could have ducked into the back alleys or surreptitiously slipped into the twist and gotten there unhassled by Hylics

— they just never got it — but who knew what I'd be harried by instead. Best stick to the surface streets.

"You rely too much on brute force," I whispered to my shadow once we were alone.

"That's rich coming from the man throwing around enough metaphysical muscle to ripple the Berenstein Bears right out of reality," Asher harrumphed. *"On camera!"*

I fell silent, thinking. If I was the cause, I had to do something about it. I'd been lamentably passive of late — a passenger in my own life, I felt. Just floating along with the jetsam of the world. Reactionary.

Time to take charge.

I knocked thrice on the Remembrancer's door.

"So what's your grand plan then?" Maybe I could get some classic villain monologue action. Kill the time until Felix showed up. Or I figured out how the hell I was being kept here.

"Felix dies," the alchemist remarked offhandedly, standing in front of the niche next to me, twisting a parrot feather twixt gloved fingers. "Balance restored." Deep thought.

"That simple, huh?"

"Oh, no, far from it," Fulcanelli shifted eyes to me. "There's nothing *simple* about felling one such as he. If it can even be done," the bastard at least doubted. That gave me a little hope.

Fulcanelli raised a hand — some sort of signal — and the cathedral organ played a note. I'd heard it a few times since I'd come to, but only when the alchemist approached one of the etheric cages. Some sort of control?

The sound drowned out whatever had transpired next to me, but the feather was gone now.

"No, no, still not enough…" Fulcanelli fussed over the task.

"What's with the noise?" I'd try another stall tack — boys love explaining their toys.

"Simple force field," Fulcanelli tapped on the invisible wall. "Teluric harmonics tuned to the sacred geometries. Fascinating really," the alchemist fell for it. "Grand cathedrals such as these are built on resonant places of power and when one is initiated into the mysteries of matter and mind, it all becomes so clear."

Fulcanelli paced in thought while speaking — churning over whatever mystery eluded his grasp as the words fell out.

"I've spent no small part of my life studying such places," he stroked the masonry. "They're rife with secrets. Like those windows," his eyes climbed higher to the stained glass. "You see the miraculously rich reds and blues?"

"Sure." They were pretty, but I wouldn't say miraculous.

"For near three hundred years, the secret of their make was lost." Let the pontification begin.

"Until you found it?" I jumped the gun.

"No," he admitted. "My teacher." Ah. I doubted the asshole had ever actually accomplished anything on his own.

"Didn't he teach you how *not* to be a total prick?"

"And here I thought you'd like to learn the mysteries yourself," Fulcanelli sighed. "I know you've an affinity for architecture. You'd make a fine student."

Ew. No.

"Not interested in your oppression and oligarchy, kay-thanks-bye," I turned my back on the creeper, focusing on the lacy carvings lining my cell walls — graved pages of a book. "All I see written in these stones is fear. Ugly, shitty, fear."

"Fear, you say?" The alchemist laughed. "Of course there's fear! It's the only thing Hylic simpletons understand — fear the Divine lest they meddle where they ought not."

"With your power, you mean," I broke out the scoffs. Good one, too — put my full body into that one. Back arched, hip kicked out as it traveled up my spine and out my flared nostrils.

"If only you could see," the alchemist lamented. Fanatic. "Such a waste."

Oh how I wished I could wipe that better-than-thou look off his smug face.

"DeWitt," the parrot joined in, albeit weakly. It sounded strange in its cage — pained. Must have been why it was mostly quiet of late.

Would that I fucking well could, I kept to myself, wondering if the parrot had read my thought.

"Ah, it's revived again, our little bird of Hermes," Fulcanelli turned toward the cage. Heels clipped on the marble floor as the alchemist stalked toward the gilded cage. "Shall we feed our little auspice again?"

Goddamn fucking rat bastard scavenger had to be stopped.

Well, I tried to.

Unexpectedly, it swung inward of its own volition.

"Come in, sweetie," the Remembrancer beckoned, kneading biscuits in a bowl. Gone was the knock-off Italian restaurant masquerading as a strip joint of dubious cuisine and instead a simple — homey, even — kitchen where she put the dough in a greased pan. "I've been expecting you," she smiled like everyone's favorite aunt, put them in to bake, and wiped her floured hands on the oven towel.

The heat was not unpleasant as it kissed my skin after the chill walk. Ruth carefully placed apron on hook, revealing her immaculately kept dress of blue silk embellished with pearls, and sat with me at the kitchen table.

"No Goff?" I noted the lack of bodyguard.

"Do I need him?" Ever to the point, her clear eyes awaited an earnest answer. I keep expecting her to one day be surprised by what I say, but it's not happened yet. Everything in stride, every possibility counted.

"No, ma'am." Though I didn't quite think she ever actually needed him. Probably had the metaphysical equivalent of a forty-five in that bag of hers all the time. Sweet old lady she may appear, but I'd think thrice before I ever crossed her if I were you.

"It's good to see you," she patted my arm. "How can I help?"

I didn't bother asking if there were any changes — the path may have slightly altered, but the outcome was the same. I felt confident she'd have led with a second option if one had come up — she did like me, after all. I was pretty sure.

"Come to square a few things," I opened the bag I'd lugged about. "Set some others right. Prepare for," I paused, "you know."

"For when the bell tolls," she squeezed my hand gently — the reassuring warmth bolstered my resolve. I needed it — there were a *lot* of amends to make, this life and next.

"So here," I went on, pulling out the first bit — a pair of horseshoes: one silver, one iron. "For back rent."

The Remembrancer's large eyes took in Nemli's wardings. What? The cabin was *on fire!* I'd pay him back.

"Perfect," she smiled. "Let me get your painting," she moved for her purse.

"That," I settled another debt, "goes to another, if you'd be so kind. For a debt long owed, recently recalled."

"Of course, sweetie." She knew all the debts everyone kept, but never niggled at you unless they'd come due. She always had faith you'd do the right thing and was rarely let down. "A debt repaid in kind," she marked off her mental ledger. "What else?"

I handed her a packet of letters. Some had instructions. Others held only fond memories to relive again. And one held a C-note with the words 'They do still exist. Be careful.'

"Wouldn't it be better, delivering those yourself?" She fussed about her bag a bit, shifting things around as she tucked the goodbyes away.

"No time," I smirked slightly, sliding the final parcel across the table — a cleverly wrapped box, faintly ticking. "I've a lot to do. And they wouldn't understand."

"So I see," she chuckled. "For Molly, I presume?" I nodded.

"This, too," I handed her the largest envelope to go with the box. "She'll need them."

"She needs you." Dagger right to the heart.

"I know, that's why I'm going," I mustered my roguish charm. "One way, remember?" I held up a single finger as I smiled.

"Oh, sweetie," Ruth grabbed my hand once more, her eyes wet. "Good luck," she squeezed. "Both of you," she added to my shadow.

"Now," she moved to other business. "Let me fix you a plate to go."

"That's a girl," Fulcanelli cooed to the cell next to mine. "Eat every bit up so you grow big and strong!"

"I thought the bird was important," I tried to wrap my head around what was happening. "Akashic Index or something."

"The bird's fine," he assured me. "It'll come back," he waved a red feather at me, then placed it in the cage. "Annoying as ever."

The alchemist was nuts. Well, they all have been a little, from what I could tell — must be the mercury — but this nut bar took the cake.

"Just you wait," he called to the ginger fairy next to me, "I've got a special treat for you next."

Shit.

"Not you," Fulcanelli rolled his eyes. "It's already drunk from you," his turn to scoff. "No need to waste any more soul than that on a weapon."

"It's a living creature," I shot back. "The fucking bitch," still not forgiving it, but it *was* alive.

"That *fucking bitch*, as you put it, is indeed a singularly unique creature," the alchemist's smile was dangerous. "One I most graciously thank you for placing in my path.

"A stroke of great luck, in fact," he went on. "Ironic, that. Felix tried, through his blood, to have it assassinate me in the Scriptorum..."

"Pity she failed," I grouched.

"…but instead gave me the perfect weapon against him!" Yep, nutbar was monologuing now. "Our little austice here has fed from an ensouled Obfirmata, the blood of Felix, thrice upon the bird of Hermes…" I guess that was the parrot? "…who knows what before we even arrived at the Scriptorum, and upon mine own self."

At this last, he removed the obnoxiously round sunglasses and hat, showing his scars from the ginger fairy's kiss. Not only was his hair now entirely white like mine had been, his eyes were completely blank as well — no irises, no pupils, nothing but smooth white shot through with blood.

"And now," he hummed a resonant note, deactivating one of the cells. "Upon death itself."

I'd never heard the nauseating noise they made before, not truly. My ears had always sort of filled in the yips and the light barks where the sounds should go just like my eyes saw the fluffy red as friend-shaped.

The unearthly keen that followed Fulcanelli from the cell, cage in hand, could not begin to register in my brain as my eyes tried to twist sideways out of my head.

"That's not a fox," was all I could manage.

"No, it certainly is not," malevolent glee filled the mad alchemist's eyes.

A Timeless Light

IT WAS ONE OF those days I just felt like crying.

Where the masks are broken and the walls crumble.

All too much slamming me at once.

I wasn't sure what was going on. Too distracted.

It happens, more than I'd like. I'm in the middle of... something... and the waves of sorrow roll in and I have to pick back up with just a few words.

"Felix?" No response.

"Felix...?" Again. With a shoulder shake.

"Asher?" An urgent whisper, afraid of the answer.

I wasn't too sure myself, but the unease in Molly's voice brought me round. Where had she come from? I was coming to find her.

"No, it's me," I said eventually, still slightly glazing.

"Me who?" Fair question. Eyebrow raised.

"His Egregious Lordship Edmund, Bishop of Dolloway," slipping some truth, guised as snark. I tried to stand, placing my hand on tumbled stone. Looked like my walls weren't the only thing broken. "Where..."

"Move!" Before I could, Molly yanked me to the side.

Good thing, too, since the wall above us exploded, adding to the rubble I'd been sitting in. How'd that happen? Nothing made sense.

Like... well shit.

"Fucking logovore," I spat.

"There he is," Molly turned my face to hers. "Glad to have you back."

"Where's my shadow?" I noticed its disturbing lack, now that I was aware. Even in the dark, we cast a shadow, murky as it may be mingling with others.

"Fighting *that*," she gestured vaguely, "what you just called it. Clocked you pretty good." Her face resumed concern.

"Logovore," I held my hand to my head — came back bloody. "Eats reason and logic." Phages to the left of me, vores to the right. "You know that ancient Chinese curse?"

"May you live in interesting times?" That was one.

"No, the other," I grimaced. "May you find what you're looking for."

It'd found me first.

I came alone under a timeless light. A light that kept following me, most annoyingly.

"Could you stop?" I shot a glare up at the moon. Stalker.

Round and full, it hung there laughing at me just above the horizon.

"Don't go dissing Luna," Asher rippled in my shadow, drinking in the beams spilling over the pavement, growing larger and more well-defined. "You know she means well."

She wasn't the only one.

I stared at the sword crossing my shadow's step at the waist, feeling the awkward absence at my own. How long had I carried it? Centuries?

When you've eliminated that which is impossible, whatever remains — no matter how improbable — must be true.

That's how the quote went, and that's what the blade did — eliminate the impossible. I flexed my hand, remembering the touch of the world flayed in flux.

Too much.

"Head in the game," my shadow whistled my attention. "Spot's just up ahead."

No other shadows danced that I could see and I felt no ripples indicative of traps or glamours or shit I just didn't want to deal with. The cathedral was on the old side, for the States, tucked in between some less decrepit buildings.

The stained glass was gorgeous, lit from within — coalter blue glowing rich with alchemy. No wonder he'd chosen this place — there was power laid into its very bones. No convenient lightning bolts lit the night in search of enemies, though I saw the shadows of gargoyles and grotesques ready to carry any rains away from the stone edifice.

"Smash them all," Asher counseled, ever ready for the introduction of violence.

"Hush you. I got in trouble for that already." I flipped my collar up against the wind's bite.

"Well do something instead of just walking into a trap." My shadow stopped keeping pace, stubbornly refusing to move.

"But I already know it's a trap as I'm walking into it, so I'm already better off than walking into it unaware." Perfect sense.

"*How* are you better off?"

"Moral high ground?" I shrugged and drug my shadow along, stamping my heel thrice to snap him to.

"That's some bullshit," his hand went habitually to the hilt at his hip.

"Usually all I've got to work with," I clanged the iron door knocker.

The door I stood in front of was rather large, massive one might say if they'd done the calculations. It seemed to be made entirely of thick sawn barn timbers all riveted together with wrought bands. Yet, it swung silently inward as in the distance an organ struck an ominous chord, rendering the oaken slab seemingly weightless.

"Creepy," my voice carried in echo.

"Astutely observed as always," Fulcanelli drolled. "Did you bring the ring?"

"Secret of my success," I snarked. "Blanket statements for the win." I spread my hands wide and gave my most roguishly disarming grin. "And yes," I produced the memento of St Germain with a flourish, walking forward to hand it over.

"Ah," the alchemist drew a line of pink smoke with a lit Bidi. "You can stop right there. Throw it."

"Oh," I looked down at the marble floor, pointing at a suspicious edging. "Is this where the trap door is? Or am I meant to stand under an anvil," I looked up, "or perhaps you've some poisoned darts trained on me from the shadows?"

I crossed the line.

"Last warning," Fulcanelli sang-song, accompanied by the demented pipe organ.

Inspired by the absurdity of the moment, I did a little dance. Wished I were makin' a little love. And got down just in time to avoid the pink stream of smoke that sliced right where my head had been.

It wafted harmlessly off the wall behind me as soon as it'd passed over, but make no mistake — there'd been a razor's edge to it. Guess he still didn't like me.

"F-sharp?" I couldn't help it. I was in a whole-ass mood.

The bastard smirked ever so slightly. Not the crack-of-a-smile smirk that meant a joke, however punny, had landed, but rather the well-wearied smirk of a man who's had to endure such attempts at humor for the very last time.

"B-flat," he sang again, this time an invisible wave of pressure swept me into an ornate column. Which kinda hurt in and of itself — the impact sent the ring clattering from my grasp — but the pointy angel wings ornamenting the base were really digging into my kidney.

Might need that for just a bit longer, so I was grateful when the note ended, and, with it, the pressure.

"See," I gloated. "You *can* appreciate a well crafted pun," I straightened my jacket after I dusted myself off the floor. "There's the ring," I nodded at where it'd landed. "Now where's Molly?"

"What? No banter begging how my powers work? No awe at the glorious might of alchemy?"

"Nope," I wouldn't give him the satisfaction. "In fact, I already know and have taken care of the problem." My shadow had, anyway, slipping quietly away as I distracted.

"You should have died when you had the chance!" Fulcanelli connected some dots as he gestured with the cigarette — a stabbing motion.

Nothing.

Again the alchemist gestured — this time another slash. Again, nothing.

I squicked a little at what I knew Asher would have done to whatever was playing the notes. Trying not to let it show, I walked forward — smile maniacally wide.

The shadow carried a sword, I thought, as it flashed by — briefly stopping to look through each arch. I followed it as best I could — see what the hell was going on. Fulcanelli had disappeared after he'd fed the not-a-fox to the ginger fairy next door. I could see its body limp below the parrot's cage — fur now bleached arctic white as all its colors had been drained away. Discarded like the bird, who still hadn't risen again.

I pressed up against the invisible field keeping me confined — I'd discovered I could just barely see the organist if I essentially stuck my eyeball right up to the corner.

Wish I hadn't — the shadowed sword struck, parting head from body in a spray of black. Sound muffled a few feet beyond the field, so I couldn't hear the head speak, though the mouth moved.

"Would you like to buy a bo..." the imp's face contorted trying to say *book*. I recognized it from the labyrinth, though why it was here playing the mad alchemist's pianist, I couldn't tell you. Had they been in cahoots all along?

I'd have loved to ask, had the shadow not followed up on its slash with a downward stab, skewering the imp's head.

I pounded on the field, rippling the air to gain the shadow's attention. Whose was it? What was it doing here? The uncanny creature turned toward my cell and rose to an imposing height — well clear of a standard six feet, but not quite seven — Sassy still had it beat.

"Get me out!" *Whoever you are.* I'd left my shadow with Hank at the Last Chance, but it was nothing like this. Had Felix called in reinforcements? Was someone else pissed at Fulcanelli? If so, they could damn well get in line.

"Hey!" I called as it turned to go. Trying to make eye contact with a shadow is hard, but I looked it in whatever passed for its face — though I felt a tad swimmy in my head.

It puffed up and exhaled, rather dramatically.

"Was that a sigh?" I kicked out my hip. The nerve. "Don't *sigh* at me. Get me out!" I punched the field for emphasis.

The shadow held up a hand and pointed to my cell before flickering away.

Rude. What? Was I supposed to wait here quietly?

Fuck that.

I'd had all the *saving* I could stomach.

I quested out with my senses, spreading fingertips over the stone surrounding me, seeking the smallest purchase, the slightest crack through which to send the slimmest root.

Resonant power binding all as one rebuked my efforts — whatever telluric energy enabled the force field coursed through the entirety of the cathedral walls as well.

I'd tried twisting out, to no avail — just meant I couldn't read the words engraved in my cell. Well, let me clarify — it meant the words no longer worded, looked like scribbles. Even when the letters behaved themselves, I couldn't read it. Some form of bastard Latin, I'd guess. Either way, the walls were just as solid, twisted or not. Strike two.

Next! I pulled the hag stone from my pocket. Perhaps peeking through the ethereal would give me some sort of hint. Through the hole in the rock, I *could* see the energies trapping me — they flowed through the words and all around the niche, making a circuit of sorts. Beyond the arch, I could see other glowing lines flowing throughout the cathedral in whorls and magnetic eddies that occasionally joined rushing torrents as they coursed through the stones.

Strangely, none of the lines crossed with the ones flowing around my cell — those were isolated. Cut off.

I felt an idea forming. If I could arc the gap, join the currents, it may...

White fur shuffled out the corner of my eye. I thought. I reached out to the poor creature, feeling for signs of persistent existence. I'd never felt the not-a-foxes before, not like the other inhabitants of the wood. There was a distinct *absence* to them — a void I dare not stare into — where the spark of life should be.

Here was no different, yet now I could recognize that void, that chill, that utter absence after meeting Thousand-Winters.

Death, incarnate in some small aspect. Utterly still and unmoving in the bleached body.

"Who are you? You who has worn the glofa of my kin," the not-a-fox said in my head, one beady eye opening.

"The hell is a glofa?" My mouth ran ahead as my brain tried to catch up. "Oh! The foxgloves. How'd you know?" At least my mouth knew better than to give my name.

"You've the scent upon you," the voice was weak, but growing stronger. I looked at the not-a-fox through the hag stone, seeing black tendrils creeping toward it from the skewered imp's head. *"Trusted by the grave."*

I mean, maybe? Calley did seem to like me when Felix wasn't around — though I suspected she just wanted to get him back. I felt the flask she'd filled from beyond the gate sitting in my pocket.

"What are you?" I had to ask — know thy terrors and they may diminish.

"We watch," it whispered. A second eye opened and the not-a-fox turned more fully toward me. If you didn't know there were too many, often glowing, you'd be hard pressed to tell the extra eyes were there, shut as this one's were.

"We watch all who elude death's grasp," it stood, the too-many eyes trying to open. *"And wait."*

"Cool, cool," I tried not to creep out. "Well how about instead of just watching, you help me out of here?"

The not-a-fox considered for a moment, tail swishing in thought.

"I did help one of you out before, you know." Well, I'd thought it was just a baby fox trapped under a bucket. Little did I know then. But hey, favor is a favor.

"We watch," it said. *"We do not interfere."*

"Seems to me, you're the one that's been interfered with," I pointed out. Revenge is a great manipulator.

The death spirit stared at me, each eye blinking individually in a ripple that carried into its hackles as they raised.

"How?'

"First off," I smirked. "You know how to play the piano?"

"Can't you do anything for yourself, Champ?" Time for the mind-fu. The figment of St Germain had clued me in to the con.

The fake froze, smoke streaming from the fancy cigarette. I wondered who that particular affectation had been stolen from.

I kept walking forward, closing the gap while waiting for Asher to return.

"All this," I waved around the magnificent cathedral, "someone else's work. You just took up residence like some sort of hermit crab. You don't even have your own name," I spat. "Have to tread on someone else's." Rile the bastard up, it's what you do with super-villains.

"I *am* Fulcanelli," he fumed where he stood. "I *am* the Last Alchemist!" Good froth, keep working it up. "I'm the only to perfect the Projection Powder and..."

"Only to *finish* it," I interrupted. "You didn't figure it out, just followed some instructions. Good at that, I'll admit," I ran my toe along some intricate details inlaid into the floor. "Deciphering the manuals hidden in plain sight. Bringing the work of others to fullness."

Bad habit of the alchemists. Stupid inquisitions made it necessary. Can't secret it away, no one would ever find it. Can't openly pass on the knowledge — that led straight to the bonfire. Had to be clever about it so that all could potentially see, though there was no guarantee those able to figure it out were — well, not total scumbags. Like this one.

"I knew something was off about you." Rakozy had been right. I remembered the real Fulcanelli, if but briefly. Kinda in that fuzzy area of my head. He'd been kind of an ass, but nothing like this facsimile. "You kill him and take over the nom de guerre? Or did he fail in..." I motioned to his presentation.

"The Divine Union? Yes," the pretender bit. "I watched as his skin sloughed from his bones, unable to coalesce into perfection. His will too weak."

Credit for that. Had to admire the tenacity. Couldn't say it though, not while the asshole was still trying to kill me. But why hadn't Fake-anelli made a move for the ring? It was just two steps in front of him.

"You're perfect then?" Narcissus much?

"Once," a smirk. And a... ripple?

Fucker. Double fake.

I tensed, scanning around me. Rat bastard had lured me in with a projection. No wonder he hadn't taken a step, even as I approached. Or done, well, anything besides gesture.

"I have to thank you though," he gloated, projection fading now that the jig was up. "You gave me the seed of your own demise."

Diva. Stolen as it was, asshole had style.

"Found her," my shadow returned. "Locked up in a cell down there next to something nasty looking."

The seed of my demise no doubt. Fun.

"Didn't want to risk letting it out with her, motioned for her to wait — she couldn't hear me," Asher paused. "She wasn't happy."

"I can imagine," I sighed.

"Dead catimeye there, too." My shadow was full of such good news.

"Not-a-fox," I grimaced. *The hell that come from?*

"Why do you do that? The silly names," Asher tangented. "I'm you and I still can't figure it out. Things have proper names, and you know most of them."

"Speaking calls," I reminded him. "And I really don't want them to have this number."

"Fair," my shadow stilled, considering. "Many things would give you trouble that cause me no pause." Damn I was full of myself.

"No duh," I glared. "Trying to keep a low profile this time around," and it wasn't working.

I sighed. Maybe after this... no, stay on task.

"Better go get her before she does something I'd do."

Violently, the cathedral shook as the organ played... well, badly.

"I thought you..." and drew my finger across my throat.

"I *did*," Asher prickled. "That creepy imp is definitely dead. Probably in on it all along," he conjectured.

"Then...?" A few more chords resounded, tinkly mixed with deep. Like a cat walking across the keys — or someone trying to find the right note.

Fuck.

"She'll tear the whole place down," my shadow alarmed, jumping to the same conclusion.

Asher ran ahead of me, shadow stretching thin beyond the light's reach. Around me the stonework lit and sparked with unnerving discord, crackling with disharmony. The stained glass rattling and shattering, letting the moonlight in.

Then stopped.

"Guess she found the right..." My relief cut short with a snarl and a scream.

The snarl? No clue.

The scream, though, that was Molly's.

I saved my breath and ran faster. She'd be okay.

She had to be.

This was definitely *not* okay.

Sure, I was out of my cell, but so was the — well it wasn't the ginger fairy anymore. That bitch was gone, replaced instead by something broken and unholy and just plain *wrong*.

Gone were its eyes, replaced by teeth — the better to eat you with. Mouth sewn shut, bulging at the cheeks and throat as if it'd gorged itself too greedily — forced to keep it in. Bent backwards and broken, it clawed itself along the marble floor — unable to walk, unable to fly — grasping the niche's edge with fingers splayed wide.

Where it touched, blackened and cracked — sparks arcing to ground from the stone. A quick peek through the hag's eye showed the eddies of telluric power coursing into its fingertips — it was feeding.

My stomach turned and threatened to revolt — just looking at it sucked all hope away — and still I couldn't look away. Its weight on the real was inescapable. The poor creature was suffering, driven mad.

"Shit, it's loose." Felix! Except, not.

Out of the cell, I could hear it now — the shadow. It rose, dark against the tumultuous sparks showering the walls. A voice like Felix's, but cold. Asher.

"Don't kill it," I preempted his strike.

"Why not?" He held the shadow of a sword pointed at the creature as it fed still, seeking an opening. "It's dangerous."

"Don't," I repeated. "Whatever it is now is not its fault. What it *was* is a ginger fairy."

The shadow tched, angling his blade more defensively.

"The one that tasted my blood?" Wary now.

"Felix's," I corrected. "Yes. Fulcanelli gave it other things to eat, too. Said he was making a weapon."

"Seed of my demise," the shadow said. "Just heard him bragging about it," he shifted, looking for an opening. "What else?"

"That parrot," I pointed over to the silent cage. "Three times, somehow. Think it's an ex-parrot now though."

"Bird of Hermes," Asher called it as well. "It'll be fine. And?"

"A not-a-fox. It's not dead though," I explained. "It helped me escape after you just left me here." Where'd it gone?

"Dead can't die again," the shadow spared me a glare. "And I told you to wait cause I didn't know how to get you out while keeping *that* thing trapped," he pointed his sword for emphasis.

"The imp could've told you," I smarmed the murderer, "but you killed it." If Asher was loose...

"The fuck is that thing?" Felix! For real this time, his face anyway. Rounding the corner and pulling up short.

"A problem," Asher, being helpful. "Big one," he readied his sword.

Before I could say anything, the world went slightly mad.

Felix to the left of me, Asher to my right in shadow, the creature had stirred and screamed not through its sutured mouth, but in my own brain. I felt sick, doubling over in terror as it sprang up, hurling itself at Felix on spindly spider legs newly grown from its stomach.

I tried. I tried, but my damn legs wouldn't move — frozen — and could only watch as the monster slammed into the man I held dear, carrying him off his feet and into the wall behind. Sparks and screams flew from the wall as it shattered around them. Gouts of flame erupted from the cracks in stone, turning to rubble that gave way to gravity.

Why? Why hadn't he tripped on a shoelace or slipped on a fucking banana peel for gods sake? His luck always held...

Until it didn't and I saw him crumple to the cold slab floor.

Unmoving.

The shadow leapt, sword swinging down on the fell creature's unprotected back. I didn't care. Kill it.

But he missed, shadowed blade striking barely a hair's breadth from Felix's own head as the creature skittered up the wall and down the hall — mind-screaming all the while.

"This is your fault," I accused. "Isn't it? Isn't it!" He'd done something to Felix's luck.

"Fix him," the shadow snapped, ignoring my rage and bolting after the attacker.

How? I wanted to shout. I pulled Felix upright, checking for a pulse — present, but thready. So thready, I had a hard time feeling it through my own.

I'd never seen him this still — never. Always fidgety or talking or scheming. Doing something. Even when I'd seen him sleeping, he never kept still — always dreaming.

"Felix?" Please.

"Felix?" Please wake up.

"F..."

He was crying.

"Come back to me, Felix." I cried, too. Our tears mingling on his cheek.

"You're working together now? You and the murderer,"
Molly took a tone just short of chiding after I'd come to.

"You worked with Bill," I countered. "Needs must," with a
shrug.

"That was different," she tried. "How'd it go with him,
anyway? Is he with you?" Molly looked hopeful. I wasn't
sure if it was because she'd grown slightly fond of the
murder-hobo during their travels or because she preferred
the goblin to my shadow.

I wasn't sure which I preferred myself.

"He had business elsewhere," I lied. "But I think things are
patched up." He'd offered — always giddy for violence — but
I still couldn't trust him. Not for this, but I'd had another job
for him.

"Look," I took a moment, holding her hand. "I know you
don't like him, but you need to understand he's me — much
as I hate it," I grimaced. Oh, how I hated it. "The parts I tried
to bury and forget in the Lethe, sure. But still me."

"I know," she deflated a bit, gripping my fingers tight. "But
the asshole has absolutely *zero* redeeming qualities!"

"That's how it goes," I couldn't help but laugh. "He's
everything I'm not," I started.

"Tell me about..." she started to gripe.

"I am," I lifted her chin. "He's everything I'm not," I
repeated, "and *I'm* everything *he's* not," I kissed her.

"So," she reasoned, kissing me back. "That makes you
everything I want."

I stole a moment to linger in that perfect moment of timeless light — a memory to remain untouched forever after.

"When this is done," Molly looked up at me, eyes glistening. "I want you to promise me you'll drink this," she said, placing a stainless flask in my hands.

I quirked an eyebrow. Not quite the way I thought that sentence would finish.

"What is it," I sniffed the flask, recognizing it instantly. "Why…?"

"Perfect," my shadow returned, logovore in tow. "You're awake!" Asher caught a swipe from the creature's talons on his sword, deflecting it in a shower of sparks that seemed to diminish the blade. "Help me kill this thing." It'd grown again, sharper, more defined in its terror.

"And you," he addressed Molly. "Don't try to stop us this time, cupcake. It's unraveling reality around itself." He leapt back, dodging a stab from one of the thing's spindly legs.

"Thought you'd be able to handle it yourself," I jabbed, pocketing the flask for later. "Gimme two seconds." I turned back to Molly.

"Felix?" I didn't know what her plan was or why she had the waters, but I could guess.

"It's okay, Molls," I had to grin. "Be seeing you."

Asher couldn't do it alone, neither could I. Even working together was a maybe. But there was a third option.

I turned toward my fate. No more running away.

All around, the power of the cathedral was running amok, spilling free from the proper channels to wreak havoc as the logovore devoured all the knowledge imbued within the structure by the masons and alchemists — growing stronger by the second.

Thing was, I was me. And a reality being set to frothy boil gave me so, so very much to work with.

Time for my biggest cheat yet.

The logovore had Asher locked down, slippery as he was in shadow — the rules no longer strictly applied.

That just wouldn't do, so I nudged a few things in my favor — causing a confluence of stray energies to form just above my pinned shadow.

And build. Build until the wall glowed lava hot, beginning to melt — dripping on the logic eater with searing pain. It arched back and Asher stabbed out, piercing its bloated side with the shadowed blade — still diminishing with each strike.

I clenched my fist and struck my heel thrice on the floor — drawing my shadow back to me like a magnet. The spindly legs still had him trapped even as they skittered in pain, but not for long. Lava rock began to bubble and swell above the two, no longer dripping.

"Do it!" My shadow screamed as it drew thinner and thinner, unable to resist my summons.

My hand opened, allowing the building pressure to burst all at once — right into the logovore, sending it flying across the room covered in molten stone. Asher snapped straight back to me — the recoil enough to clear him of the micro eruption.

Free from the forces coursing through the walls, the makeshift lava hardened around the logovore.

"Is it...?" Molly ventured from the wings.

"No," though I wished it was. "That only slowed it down. Bought me some time."

"Time for what?" Molly was nervous — well she should be.

I knelt and closed my eyes, setting my shadow to boil in the timeless light cast from within — the very stuff of me.

Asher ran ahead, the essence of shadow roiling to a boil, rising from the stones in tendrils of black steam — I sprinted after, feeling the air thicken around me.

"Felix!" Molly cried after me. I couldn't stop. Not now.

"Go!" I screamed as I ran toward the silhouette rising from the ground ahead of me. "Get the bastard who started this shit." I didn't want her to see this me. Didn't want to imperil her soul. But she wouldn't have gone, not unless there was reason. "I'm right behind you."

I took one last look as myself before plunging into my abyssal shadow.

I knew Felix was different — hard not to — but until that moment, I hadn't realized just *how* far from the norm he truly was.

And then he was gone.

Swallowed by the shadow he cast, emerging from the other side changed — taller, broader, his movements less fluid but more sure — commanding. Drawn sword held high, he charged the logovore as it struggled to free itself from the crusted earth.

"Go," he ordered — voice like neither Felix nor Asher. One used to being obeyed without question.

I resisted the urge to mount a snarky comeback, biting my tongue. Deep inside the echo of Dena cautioned calm, gently suggesting perhaps leaving the heart of the maelstrom to come, lest I cause greater tragedy.

Simply put, I was out of my league and I knew it.

Shadow draped his form, drinking away the light as he struck the rocky cocoon trapping the monster — sword plunging deep, cloak billowing wide with the swing giving him the appearance of wings. He looked up to me, his face, too, masked in creeping shadows though his eyes showed through — they glowed red.

This is what they feared. This was the reason everything that went bump in the night steered clear — or acted a fool out of maddening terror.

I turned.

I had my own fight to finish.

"How's ya boi," startled me from beneath a fallen capital. Guess it wasn't an ex-parrot after all. The cage was nearly crushed, but the bird seemed intact. Actually in better shape than when last I saw it — no longer looking like a plucked duck.

"Busy trying to save us all," I wouldn't look back, though I heard the terrors clashing. "Let's get you out of there," I shoved the column-top off the bent cage.

"DeWitt, DeWitt," the bird cheered.

"I am," I yanked open the door. Stubborn bastard didn't want to budge, but I was in a mood and used a bit more force than necessary — popping the lock and bending the bars around it.

"How's ya boi," the parrot squawked, flapping to my shoulder.

"He'll be fine," I assured the... whatever it was. Like the not-a-fox, I couldn't get a read on it the normal way. Would just have to make do with the bird's limited vocabulary and guessing. "Now, if I were a rat bastard fake, where would I hide?"

"Not very well," the not-a-fox returned. *"Follow."*

Flashes of white fur darted ahead down the hall as the parrot calmly rode on my shoulder. Occasionally the cathedral shuddered with impacts from the battle behind, setting the lights to rattle and shadows to dance.

It was during one of these I heard the tell-tale scream of a coward, distracting me from the motion I thought I'd seen.

It was pitiful, to be honest. The once great Fulcanelli — so haughty and proud — hid beneath a child's desk in what appeared to be a Sunday school as debris clattered down from the ceiling. At least, what was left did.

"Serves you right, asswipe," I crossed my arms in the doorway. Gaunt now, feeble and weak, the alchemist cringed at my voice — apparently unable to see. "Your little monster have you for a snack?"

"It...it," he struggled. "It disobeyed. How? How could it?"

"Here's a reality check," I snarled. "Who you want me to make it out to? I know you're not the real deal."

"I...I..." Words failed as empty eyes sought salvation.

"Nevermind, you don't even deserve a name." I stalked close, dragging the bastard from under the desk. "You reap what you sow. Living things aren't toys or experiments," I ground my teeth, "or weapons for petty revenge. You got a problem with someone, sort it out yourself. You worthless piece of shit."

"My powder," he wheezed. "My powder, please," he clutched at me before going limp. "The ring was empty, so empty."

Powder? Was that like StG's elixir?

"*Akin,*" the not-a-fox in my mind. "*Prolongs his life untouched by my kind. It runs out, yet still I cannot take him,*" it growled.

"So what do we do?"

"I *cannot*," the voice in my head menacing. *"But with the glofa..."* it left the suggestion hanging.

"DeWitt," the bird egged, flapping energetically.

Touch *that* maligned and offensive soul?

I felt all desire for vengeance leave. This pathetic piece of shit wasn't worth it.

The not-a-fox felt my decision, releasing an unearthly keen that sent shivers up my spine.

"We should depart," the suggestion was strong. *"I simply wanted to offer you first rights in courtesy."*

"Thanks," I kicked the crumpled bastard once more for good measure — square in the ribs. "I'm good," leaving the fake to his sins.

"How's ya boi?" That was really getting old.

But I'd really like to know.

"You know she means to kill us, right?" Two halves working as one — same body, shared mind, nearly complete — Asher and I fought.

"The claws and the teeth coming in such close proximity kind of gave it away," I countered another strike. "Yes."

"I meant cupcake," Asher ground and pounded the logovore in the face. "She's up to something."

"Oh that. Yeah, she is." I hadn't told him about the flask, secreting it away before he could notice. Those particular skills were all mine. "I told her to."

"Why?" I felt Asher's shock through our connection. We hadn't fully integrated, the separation still ran deep, but the borders were growing fuzzy.

"In case you got out again." Blunt, drawing on his sword skill for a riposte.

"Ouch," Asher, taken aback. "You really don't like yourself."

"Jokes on her," I rolled under a broad swipe, ignoring the psychoanalysis. "Bitch here might beat her to it."

If memory served, it shouldn't have been necessary — the dodging — something untoward should have happened to the beast for enacting violence. But for this creature, logic need not apply — even my own particular brand of it.

"It'll be close," Asher admitted. "That thing is pretty juiced," he stabbed a glancing blow. "Maybe the lava *wasn't* a good idea."

"How was I supposed to know it'd come out upgraded?" I was just trying to roast the fucking bitch. Instead it'd burst out of the rock changed, like a moth from its cocoon.

Sleeker and refined — more like the faen it'd been, just ashen and ink spill. Like a manuscript consigned to the flames of ignorance. Gone were the awkward lumps of gorging, the sutured mouth, and the spindly legs — the overt terrors given way to innate horror in its very presence.

"Alchemy 101," Asher stopped short of adding *duh*. "*Prima materia* plus crucible times heat equals *that*. Didn't you ever listen to Rakozy?"

"I kinda tuned him out after a few decades," I laughed in the logovore's face — again trying to eat mine — and kicked it off.

I nudged a few things, black mantle flaring wide to suck up the luck, and cheated so the ceiling collapsed right where the bitch would land. The improbable sword grew warm in my hands, encountering resistance at the threads of fate.

The ceiling collapsed as planned, but at the same time, a column toppled to land perfectly underneath, sheltering the logovore as it sprawled across the floor.

"I'm getting tired of that," I grumbled, readying for the creature's return. "You can bring down a big ass bridge, but a little bit of ceiling is too much?"

"It came down right," Asher defended. "Just got nudged the wrong way, like everything else we tried."

"It should still work a little even if its reality is bent." I was getting tired of nothing making sense. Fucking logovores. "And how're its attacks getting nearly through? It's not playing fair," I feigned a pout.

"It is the monster at the end of all time — a maddening glimpse of it," Asher pointed out. "It has no reason to play fair. Plus," he went on. "It's drunk your blood, fool," Asher glared in my mind. "It knows all your tricks." We braced as it sprinted from the rubble. "And some of mine. And a lot of other things to boot."

I pivoted like a matador, trying to blind it with shadow as the blade came round to bite it in the ass — and slipped.

"Not to mention the wee bit of cupcake's chaos that started all this mess," Asher's refined reflexes turned the slip into a backflip, landing square face to face with the snarling vore.

"But what if it forgot?" Oof, my epiphany distracted me as it spun a back kick at my face. It was learning, no longer acting on sheer impulse.

Awkwardly — and incompletely — dodged, I let the force back me up, sliding through the bits of broken cathedral littering the floor until I could stand.

"I don't think a knock to the head's going to do it, bud," Asher brought up the sword, seeking the improbable to slice open new possible. "And it doesn't seem game for hypnosis."

"How about a drink?" I pulled the flask, fending the logovore's claws off with the sword.

"You want to rizz your way out of this?" Cringe. Never should have let him on the internet.

"Don't ever say that again." My humor and word play was bleeding across to him as his skill was to me. Heck of a trade — I felt I got the better end of that deal.

"What?" We skipped back as the logovore pressed, slapping away the claws with our blade. "It means charisma, doesn't it?"

"Yes, I think, but it's still just *wrong*." Knowing the words doesn't always impart the nuance.

"I'll have you know we've always been a bleeding edge linguist." I did recall that — still put it into practice. "Even gave Bill that bear line, among some others." Words are fun.

And this abomination in front of us ate them. It'd retreated a wary step, unable to force through our defense.

"What's with the flask?" Asher asked in the pause.

"Present from Molly," I felt the rue rise. "Lethe's waters." She'd asked me to forget. Her, everything. I wasn't sure if she knew it'd wipe everything else along with Asher, and hadn't been able to ask.

"Well then," Asher whistled. "How're we gonna play this?"

"Splish splash, maybe?" Hell if I knew. Would be better if it'd drink it, but pretty sure the only thing it wanted to eat or drink was my... welp, figured I'd have to do something stupid. "Take the fall," I said.

"Do what?" We'd reached a near stalemate — neither of us gaining or losing advantage. The logovore'd been prowling, cautious, seeking an opening to strike. We'd give it one.

"Bait it," I flipped open the flask. "Make it good." I took a long swig, hoping I wouldn't go blank then and there. It'd taken a while the last time, I thought. Maybe it'd be long enough to pull this off.

Asher was clever about it. Subtle. Good man. He surreptitiously snipped the strand that would counter the vore's strike, allowing the creature to pounce after a few seconds. Still holding a raised guard, he stepped too wide and let it slip a fraction in the gamble.

I was just along for the ride at that point, focusing on my carnie trick — usually used for breathing fire. I couldn't cheat — it was wise to that. Watching. So it was down to pure, unadulterated luck — his bad, and my good.

A single bolt, sheared in the chaotic destruction of the cathedral, dropped to the marble floor, breaking the tension.

The logovore made the first move, tensing to spring left. We let it, bringing the blade up a little too shallowly — enough to avoid death a bit longer, but not the full force of the blow that followed.

Rolling backwards, we came to a knee, planting the sword before us while the bitch pressed its advantage, careening into my shared body and sending us in a tumbled sprawl.

Asher tried to recover — a bit too fast though, so I slowed his roll. Just enough for the vore to pin us.

Perfect. It had us pinned by the shoulders — Asher trying to work the blade around for a stab, but kept missing. Just its luck.

The logovore's tongue slathered sharp teeth, drool dripping onto my face as it looked down with empty eyes — the void incarnate. Devourer of all logic and reason and knowledge in its infinite depths.

Closer.

It savored the imminent victory.

Closer, bitch.

Its mouth opened wide to reveal row after row of spiny teeth
— nothing was getting out of that gullet. Nightmare fuel.

I spat.

Well, more expelled the waters of Lethe I held — rather
violently, this trick was meant to make a flamethrower after
all — straight into the gaping logovore's mouth.

"Now," I spat again, expunging the rest of the waters. Asher
kicked out, flinging the struggling vore off and bringing us
to our feet, ready to intercept another strike.

One that never came as the creature choked, coughing
violently as it seemed to become less than. Vile form melting
away as it forgot.

Asher raised the improbable sword for a finishing blow.

"No," I stopped him, exerting full control of will. Other
paths had opened.

"We should kill it now while it's weak!" Ever ready for
expedient violence. We'd have to work on that.

"It's no longer a threat," I held my ground as the poor
creature shrank to the ginger fairy at its core. "Put the blade
away."

Asher relented and I went to its spent little body, still
breathing, and carefully cheated the fates, just a little bit. It
hadn't been her fault. She didn't deserve this.

"I'd like to drink the colors from the leaves, please," the little
sprite perked up, fluttering to my face.

"It's a bit out of season for that, little one," I carefully said.

"Oh," it saddened.

"But your time will come again," I reassured it, pulling a cat carrier from the twist. "As with all patient things," I offered it shelter.

The ginger fairy fluttered to the door, looking into the cozy hole — reminiscent of the caves they favored, but portable. Apparently she found the moss bed I'd conjured and the unseasonal leaves acceptable and went in, pulling the door shut after — tinkling a little bell I'd placed on it to warn of escapes.

"Felix?" Molly cautiously approached, striking an odd tableau, peering around one of the less crumbled corners. On her shoulder, the bird of Hermes; at her feet, a bleached white not-a-fox.

Catimeye, Asher in my head.

Shhh, I cut him off. *Speaking...*

It's right there! He had a point. The death spirit stared at me disconcertingly. Was it smiling?

I never heard him coming.

Only the stone hand erupting from my chest gave it away. "Kinslayer," the vengeful gargoyle whispered through garbled tongue.

Molly screamed, running for me, terrified eyes locked on mine as I fell to my knees.

Thanks for saving me a trip, I thought to Gregory as he pulled his taloned fist out, eyes only for Molly.

I love you, I wanted to tell her.

But my luck had run out.

To Whom it Will Concern

"WELL THAT'S NOT OMINOUS at all," I rolled my eyes. Par for the course really.

"What's not?" Hank stopped staring into his whisky for the moment.

"To whom it will concern," I read the salutation aloud.

"Boy's always been dramatic," Hank raised his glass. "Got a flair for it."

"It is very Felix," I agreed. "Here goes." I read.

"Foreboded yet? Good! Have a drink.

"My untimely demise has no doubt set into motion some events that may become unpleasant. Sorry 'bout that. But I'm sure you'll handle it just fine. Here's the good news..."

I paused.

"...death is not as finite as what you think. Like in the Tarot, it's just a change of self and situation, clearing out the old to make way for the new. I'm probably already beyond the gate as you read this, so don't get any ideas about bringing me back. Too late for any of that," I knew.

The gloves hadn't worked. I'd tried when Gregory'd pulled his arm out and the light was leaving Felix's eyes, and... I shuddered, shoving the memory down.

"...and while I'm here I'm going to take care of some business..."

Hank hnged, likely knowing. I'd ask him later what sort of *business* required one to be deceased.

"Yes, I *am* dead. Most likely. Indubitably indisposed at the very least. You know how these things go — or you should by now. So yeah, dead. Doornail, etm."

"L. O. L. He actually said 'and shit' in Latin."

"Atta boy," Hank cheersed.

"But I saw it coming," I read on. "Well, Ruth did. She gave me the heads up and I should have told you that the 'one'..." I couldn't believe it.

"Fucker, yes you should have."

"What?" A bushy eyebrow from Hank.

"A misapprehension he let me operate under," I grit my teeth. "He knew. Asshole."

"Ah ah," Hank understood. "Does that."

Too much, I didn't add. Goes without saying.

"Try to keep yourself alive while I'm gone, okay? I've taken care of most of it, I think. Protections in place. Rents are all caught up and Ruth likes you — who doesn't, better than me anyway — so she'll help out as she can. Others, too. Hank's there. Everyone else. Maybe listen to them every now and then?"

The nerve!

"Now Missy," Hank placated. "He said nothing about *doing,* just listening."

"I'll try," I offered a smile. Tad forced.

"Just remember," I skipped ahead, "legends never die, they just change with each telling. And I am ever the Fool."

"HA!" Hank slapped his knee.

The hell did that mean?

"Thanks for the pickup, Calley," I waved bye to the death spirit on the other side of the portal.

"Long overdue," the Winter Hag smirked. "Maybe stay this time?" Yep, she'd enjoyed it. I kept waving until the tendrils of black thickened once more, sealing the Orphic door.

I flipped my coin, keeping it for myself — I knew the path by now, no guide needed. Though I'd probably stop by and say hi — maybe he needed his scythe sharpened. That grass can get quite tall, let me tell you.

But later. I wasn't taking the direct route. Not this time.

Up the hill I walked, seeking the branching rivers that flowed to the valleys of beyond. One way lay Lethe and forgetfulness, another Mnemosyne and memory beneath the poplar tree. Rivers of fire and sorrow and lamentation as well, all cut through the fields, dividing the hereafter.

Peaceful, at first blush. Pleasant. I let myself drift in the calm, relaxing.

And then everything got very quiet.

Felix Chance will return in *Ghost of a Chance*

Also By

Felixverse
Felix Chance
Second Chance
Off Chance

Science Fiction
Pandora Squad

Anthologies
"Into the Fire" in *Hidden Villains Arise*
"The Iron Sigh" in *Behind the Shadows*

Humor
98 Rabbits: An Assemblage of Words

Sign Up

My Thanks

Thank you for diving in to the world of Felix Chance. I hope I have entertained you with my words. If I have, please rate and leave a kind word or two so others may find their way to these pages.

About

j.e. pittman is an author dabbling in many speculative worlds. He blurs the borders between genre and crafts salient lies to tell a measure of truth. His work has been described as: capriciously chimeric, dreamlike, and a vivid enigma with indelible images stamped on your brain. Discover more of his words on www.halfacrepond.com

www.ingramcontent.com/pod-product-compliance
Lightning Source LLC
Chambersburg PA
CBHW060443310726
48977CB00001B/307